# First Studies in Plant Life in Australasia

This edition published 2026
by Living Book Press

Copyright © Living Book Press, 2026

ISBN:    978-1-76183-259-8 (hardcover)
         978-1-76183-248-2 (softcover)

First published in 1900.

A catalogue record for this book is available from the National Library of Australia

# First Studies in Plant Life in Australasia

*by*

William Gillies

# Contents

LEAVES OF BLUE GUM SHOWING THE OIL-DOTS (AFTER VON MUELLER).

*"Without a knowledge of plant life we may admire flowers and trees, but it is only as strangers, only as one may admire a great man or a beautiful woman in a crowd. But when one with even a slight knowledge of that delightful study goes out into the woods, or into one of those fairy forests which we call fields, he finds himself in the company of friends, every one of whom has something interesting to tell."*

– SIR JOHN LUBBOCK.

*"People think that when they have toiled for a long time, almost all their lives, that then they will come to the flowers and the birds, and be joyful in the sunshine. But no, it will not be so; for then they will be old themselves, and their ears dull and their eyes dim, so that the birds will sound a great distance off and the flowers will not seem bright."*

– RICHARD JEFFERIES.

# PREFACE

THIS book is meant for boys and girls beginning the study of plant life. It is true that I have given, wherever possible, the reason for the facts stated about plant life: a branch of the subject which is generally kept back for a senior course. I have done this because I believe that the method of keeping beginners exclusively to the facts is false to the principles of true teaching. Anyone may see this who walks into the fields with a child and takes note of the questions he puts. If you tell a child that the leaves of an elm are alternate, stipulate, pinnate, with the blade unequally divided by the midrib, he will soon grow tired; but if you lead him below an elm tree and show him that the peculiar shape of the leaves enables each leaf to catch the maximum of light, he will listen readily. Also, you have given him a key to the meaning of leaves and leaf-form that may bring him to your side with many other eager questions about other leaves. Almost unconsciously he has learned the purpose of a leaf, and this in itself helps him to understand a hundred things in the life of the leaf that were meaningless before.

Similarly, if you tell the child that a snapdragon flower is personate and bilabiate, with didynamous stamens and a two-lobed superior pistil, he will soon grow tired; but if you try to explain to him that the snapdragon's curious mouth is due to the visits of bees, he will listen readily. Also, you have given him a clue to the meaning of a multitude of strange-shaped flowers; and the endless variety of form in these flowers no longer bewilders him.

It is true that in approaching plant-life in this way we have often to say to the child: "I do not know." Sometimes, too, we have to give explanations that may need to be revised with larger knowledge. But this is no reason why the child should not have the best answer to his questions that we can give. If the boy Copernicus had not been drilled in the Ptolemaic theory of the heavens, he would have had little chance of finding out the Copernican system.

Even the ignorance that we confess may often be of value to the child. When a teacher who loves his subject admits ignorance, he does it in such a way that it is a valuable stimulus to research on the part of his pupils. In a short time, they become fellow-workers with him. The atmosphere created by this method is one to quicken research and originality; and here, indeed, we have its best feature.

The old authoritative method of teaching Botany as a series of ascertained facts with all the qualities of certainty and finality not only destroyed interest in all but a few minds, but gave no impulse to inquiry—no enthusiasm of research. The barrenness of much so-called education lies in the training of young minds to receive passively certain teachings as final; the truth being that there is no finality in science. The great discoverers were great because they verified and examined and experimented for themselves; and we do them homage not for reaching finality but because they made progress. This is why such men are often impatient with the crowd of admirers who form clubs to study their work; good as such clubs are. "If I had been content," says Ruskin, "to sit at another man's feet all my life there would have been to-day no

Ruskin societies." In no part of the world, too, is the investigating mind more needed than in this new Southern World of ours. The life-histories of many of our native animals and plants is still unknown. Fine work has been done by our pioneers in Zoology and Botany, and we are grateful for their work, but the half has not yet been told. Everyone who has looked into these things for himself has seen new paths of investigation stretching out in all directions; and the boys and girls who are now being trained to observe are to be congratulated on the wide field that lies before them. Only those plants and trees have been used that are well known both in town and country. No plants have been mentioned that are known to botanists only, or that have no popular names.

The practical aspects of plant-study for Australasian scholars have not been neglected. I have tried to show that the art of the gardener and of the farmer in manuring, watering, draining, rotation of crops, budding, grafting, and the like are all copied from Nature's methods, and are only to be fully understood when learned in this way. If to-day our fields are more productive than they were fifty years ago, it is because we have won Nature to the service of man by a loving study of her ways. It was with no thought of profit, indeed, that Linnaeus and his successors studied in garden and field. Hard-headed business men looked askance at what seemed to them elegant idleness; and yet to-day the granaries of the world are more richly stored because men like these have bent over the flowers of the field. These are the men to whom Nature loves to whisper her secrets, and it is to men of this stamp that Nature gives the power to make two blades grow where before there was but one.

It is sober truth to say that if plant-life were well taught in our schools, the produce of Australasian fields would be doubled. To statesmen who are at their wit's end to find revenue, this plan for doubling the revenue of a State may be commended.

Much of the teaching in the book has been put into the questions and exercises at the end of each chapter. Pains have been taken with these, because the information given in the book will be of little value unless there be constant personal observation, experiment, and thought.

One important result of plant-study will be an increase of interest in tree-planting. Only second to this will be the growth of a conscience in our people about the native trees that still remain to us. When people understand what a great tree means, and how even a tree fern takes fifty years to grow, they will no longer be the vandals they have been in the past.

Every teacher must have noticed that a child speaks of a plant as if it could plan and feel and even think like a human being. If we are to meet the child on his own ground, we must to some extent adopt this way of speaking. This will do no harm if the child is gradually taught, as it grows older, that the plant's power of action and change is limited by laws fixed by the Creator.

It is worthy of note, however, that a plant is able to change its form and habits in ways not dreamt of by our fathers. One of our native geraniums is the same plant that one finds in Europe, but the finer climatic conditions have enabled it to change from an annual to a perennial. Striking changes occur when some plants are taken from the interior to the coast, or from the plains to the mountains.

The changes made in flowers by the agency of insects are recorded in the rocks, and the transformations wrought upon flowers and vegetables by the gardener are before our eyes daily. Changes like these are due to the power that a plant possesses of adapting itself to its surroundings. What this power of adaptation is we do not know; we can only say that the Creator has given to the plant the power to change within certain limits. A plant is not a musical box that can play its tunes in one way and in no other. The plant can play its tune with many variations according to its surroundings. The changes made on flowers by the constant visiting of insects or by man's agency are of great interest to children; and such facts prepare them to understand the great fact that life in plant or in animal is not fixed, but, within certain limits, plastic. Many a reformer, grown weary in the task of lifting human nature, has got fresh heart from this discovery. The limits of change, narrow in the plant and animal, are wide indeed when we rise to him who has been made in the image of God.

Two conditions have to be observed by him who would improve a plant. He must find out the laws of the plant's life, and he must obey these laws. By doing this we are making our garden plants more beautiful year by year; and the day is coming when we shall attempt with the same reverent obedience to the facts to beautify the garden wherein the plants are men and women.

The introductory chapter is meant for teachers, parents, and senior scholars.

The drawings are from the pencil of Mr. Wm. Huddlestone.

W. G.

# A WALK ROUND MY GARDEN

*This introductory chapter is meant for parents and teachers.*

1. As I walk round the garden on this fine morning, I try to find out the secret of its charm. Much of the charm cannot be put into words at all; but here are one or two reasons for the keen pleasure that it gives.

2. My plants interest me because I have watched them from seed to seed. I have sowed and thinned, watered and planted; I have guarded them from weeds and from slugs. I have watched for the first flower and wondered: Will it be white or pink? I have bent over them to see the bees at work. I have shown them proudly to my friends; and in doing all this a part of my life has passed into these flowers.

3. On the face of a garden Nature writes her calendar as she writes it nowhere else. Month after month inscribes its message on tree and plant; nay, in a well-stocked garden every week has its new feature that tells the passage of the year to the lover of flowers. There is a legend that the shade of Linnaeus, on returning to his old garden from the other world, guessed the date within seven days by looking at certain flowers that were just opening. The idea is not a fanciful one. Last year the gooseberry bush beside the summer-house broke into leaf on the 20th of July. This year, on the 22nd of the month, I walked down to the bush and found that the grey thorns were almost covered with a shimmer of green! That rhubarb plant burst

through the ground on the 10th of August last year, and this year the clods were pushed aside on the 11th of the month! What wonderful timekeepers these plants are! The last week of September brought the green flowers to the elm, though as yet no leaf had shewn; and the same week saw the new green fruit-balls of the plane tree swinging side by side with the old, brown battered ones. Year after year, the willow is in full leaf in the last week of August; and on the last week in September the beautiful leaves of the plane begin to hide the winter outlines of the tree. Have you heard of the chesnut at the Tuileries that was called old *Vingt Mars* by the gardeners who had grown grey in its company? This stick marks the place where an African lily is buried. There is no sign of life to-day; but, within a week, it will throw up a flower-stem! The flower is even now on the way to keep its tryst. George Eliot has the fine thought of God calling the bead-roll of the stars, and of the stars coming out in the evening sky, one by one. Even so, the flowers obey the heavenly summons...

4. Can you wonder that the Greeks conceived of this yearly marvel as the return of the Flower-goddess from the lower world? The myths of every land and the art of every eye have added their own charm to what is perennially charming. And one never tires of it as one tires of many things. Nay, since each spring adds a new memory to old memories, the new spring comes ever with a richer fragrance. The eyes become dim, but we see with the eyes of younger days; the ears grow dull, but we hear with the ears of the boy.

5. And here we catch a glimpse of another secret of the garden's charm. The birds sing from tree and covert, so that

we think of them as our birds—and as a part of the garden. Even from the "bare, ruined choirs" of winter, we hear the birds rehearsing for the spring burst of song; and when the full chorus comes on some fine September morning, the call to the garden is irresistible. James Russell Lowell, in speaking of the early days of Harvard University—then a wattled fold on the edge of the wilderness—tells us that among the students were some red Indians who were to be trained as missionaries. They worked hard for a time at Greek and Latin; but the forest whispered to them and the first blue bird of spring whistled them back to the woods. "Oh, Sir," Lowell hears them saying to their teacher, "you hear we are called!" In the country, the magpie, in town, the thrush, are our blue birds that call us out of doors. For every man who has been brought up among trees or flowers there is some bird-note that will not be denied. "Oh, Sir, you hear we are called!"

6. They interest me—these plants—because some remind me of friends, and others take my thoughts abroad to far-off lands. I remember the day, ten years ago, when I brought home the little plant from which this rose bush grew. I often think of my friend when I look at its beautiful blooms. The dew on its buds helps to keep fresh our friendship. This plant I brought from Lake Tyers, four years ago: it recalls a pleasant holiday. And here are a dozen pansies raised from seed sent to me by a friend in Scotland. Beside these are tulips from bulbs sent out straight from Holland.

7. This little scarlet pimpernel—the poor man's weather-glass[1]—takes one straight to England. It has sprung up with

---

1     So called because it shuts up before rain.

the lawn-seed, and is trying to be at home in a strange land where rain-clouds are rare. The love lily of South Africa stands close to the belladonna lily that found its way from the Cape to England when James of Scotland was King. And here, on the border, is an acanthus that grew in Greece when sculptors were learning to give the charm of flower and leaf to their stately temples. On the fence beyond is the creeper that reminds us of the rich lands of Virginia, and, beside it, the smaller-leaved variety that came to us from Japan.

8. The scent of wall-flower draws us to a plant that reached England from the Mediterranean in the Middle Ages. This chrysanthemum carries the thought to a valley of China, and the dahlia beside it takes us to its native haunts in Mexico. It is in Mexico, too, that we find this sunflower at home. Yonder golden patch of poppies is from the foothills of California—the Californian poppy[2]. These sweet peas on the fence lead us back again from America to Europe, and we seek the old home of the sweet pea in the valleys of Sicily. This white peony is from Siberia. Did it catch its colour from the snow? It is three centuries since this lilac was carried from Persia to England.

9. That foxglove recalls the flowers that grow on the sunny side of an old moss-covered wall in Surrey, and these harebells that nod in the wind take us to a breezy down in Sussex. The tall poplar at the garden-foot takes the thought to Lombardy, and to the wide plains of Germany and France; and the plane tree on the road beyond carries one, as on a magic carpet, to the Levant. This looking-glass bush is from New Zealand, and that silky oak is from the coast of New South Wales.

2    Eschscholtzia.

10. Memories of childhood are stirred as we come to a border of violets. Cherished for itself, this beautiful flower is prized still more because it brings back the first garden of childhood and the first flower that was planted in it. Happy the child who is set over a little plot of garden ground! Whatever may happen in after-life, that first garden of childhood is a garden of Eden from which he can never be driven out. And now we pass a bed of cress, and I recall the awestruck boy who saw one morning his own name rising in living green letters from the dark earth.

11. These green shoots breaking through the ground are daffodils. They come to us in August, but they also come to us with the winds of March, because it was then that Shakespeare saw them. It was then, too, that Wordsworth saw them. Here we have come upon another clue that leads us to the secret of the garden's charm. This flower is dear to us because Shakespeare loved it, and that because Milton wrote of it.

12. But, indeed, our thoughts cannot stay within garden walls when we ask the poets to walk with us. We wander into spring fields powdered with daisies and golden with buttercups, and to forest-glades where the blue hyacinth is "like the heavens upbreaking through the earth." There are cowslips among the grass and poppies in the corn, and from the woods comes a cuckoo's call that was never heard in Australia.

13. Thus am I a citizen of the world when I walk in my garden.

14. And if the flowers take us to the ends of the earth, they also take us into times long gone by. Ages have gone to the making of a plant; and its history is written on its face if only we could read it. The smallest weed has passed through a thousand changes of soil and climate, of friends and foes, and only the All-

knowing Creator could give the full story of the meanest flower that breathes. But to us, His sons and daughters, He has given the delight of being able to spell out this story here and there. There is not a line or spot on leaf or flower but has its meaning. This is the true *language of flowers*. Happy he who can read it!

I.

# How Seeds Germinate

<u>PART I.</u>

Teachers and parents are earnestly reminded of the great importance of creating interest in each subject before a formal lesson on that subject is given. Before a lesson on Roots is given, a large number of roots of common weeds should be pulled up and examined by the child. He should be asked to say what he sees in the root before he is allowed to see with the teacher's eye; to say what he thinks before he gets the teacher's thought; to suggest his own puzzles about the root before any puzzles are thrust upon him. Then, and not till then, should the orderly lesson be given.

1. **A seed with two seed-leaves.** Two seeds lay on a shelf – a seed of wheat and a French bean. They had been forgotten for four years, and they seemed dead as the dust that lay thick upon them. Spring-cleaning came round, and they were swept out with the dust, and cast upon a garden-bed. Now the earth was dry, and the seeds lay on the ground as lifeless as when they lay on the shelf. Then came a heavy rain, and washed soil over both seeds. A week of cold winds followed; and the seeds lay still in the damp, cold ground. And then a warm wind blew and, two days after, a strange thing happened. The earth was

gently pushed aside, and a tiny green shoot thrust itself into the world of light and air! At first it shot up quite straight (see fig. 7), and looked like a solid green stem; but, after a few days, it began to unroll. A long green leaf came out; and then another, and another. It was now clear that the little green shoot was not a solid stem, but a bundle of delicate leaves wrapped tightly round one another so that they could push through the earth into the air.

2. But now the French bean also has cracked the earth, and is coming up in a green loop (see fig. 4). In a day or two the loop has risen clear of the earth; but the outer coat of the bean is still clinging to the loop. A few days more, and the loop has straightened itself into a stem bearing two fleshy green leaves, that do not look like proper leaves. Next time we pass, two little green leaves that look like true leaves have risen from between the two fleshy leaves; and now the plant is fairly started in life.

3. By what magic did these dead-looking seeds, that had been forgotten for four years[3], spring into beautiful green plants? The outsides of the seeds give no answer to the puzzle. Shall we look inside?

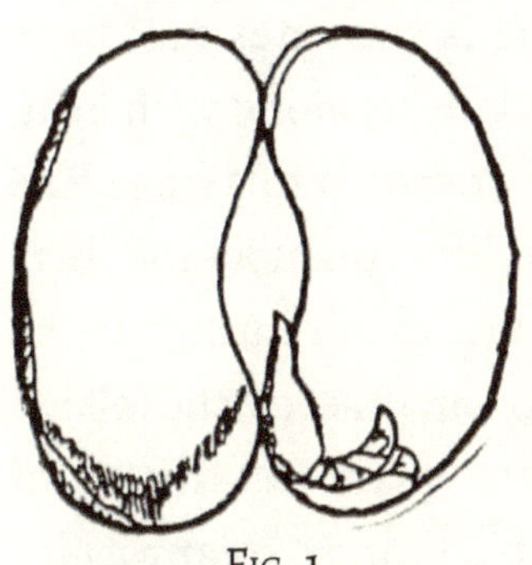

FIG. 1.
FRESH WHEAT SEED SPLIT OPEN TO SHOW THE PLANTLET.

4. **What we saw inside a French Bean:** the Plantlet. Soak some French beans for twenty-four hours. Examine a bean after it has been a few hours in the water, and you will find that the skin has puckered up into

---

3    The best seed-wheat is the wheat of the previous year. Each year added to the age makes the germination more uncertain. The stories of the germination of wheat found in Egyptian mummies are not true.

wrinkles, as if the bean's clothes were too big for it. The skin has swollen faster than the seed that lies inside it. A few hours later, the water reaches the seed within the skin, and the seed swells out and fills the skin so that it is smooth again.

5. And now use finger and nail gently and split open the bean. The seed-coat peels off, and the halves of the bean fall apart. Can these halves be the two strange green fleshy leaves that we saw on the top of the loop? They have the same shape, but are white. We shall see. Fastened to a point near the end of one of the halves, is a tiny object that looks like a little plant with the leaves bunched up. You look through your lens, and see two small leaves. They must be leaves, for you see the veins quite clearly. These, then, must be the second pair of leaves that we saw. They cannot be the first pair, for these were not veined. But all this is guess-work; so now let us make an experiment.

6. **How to watch seeds while germinating.** The simplest way of all is to grow the seeds in moist sawdust. This provides moisture and air; and these, along with heat, are the three needs at this stage. The seeds can be lifted out now and then, examined, and then returned to the sawdust. For small seeds, the following is a better plan: Get the top of an old lamp chimney, or any cylindrical glass tube open at both ends. Roll some fresh white blotting-paper into a tube, and slip it into the glass tube. Fill in, then, with loose moist

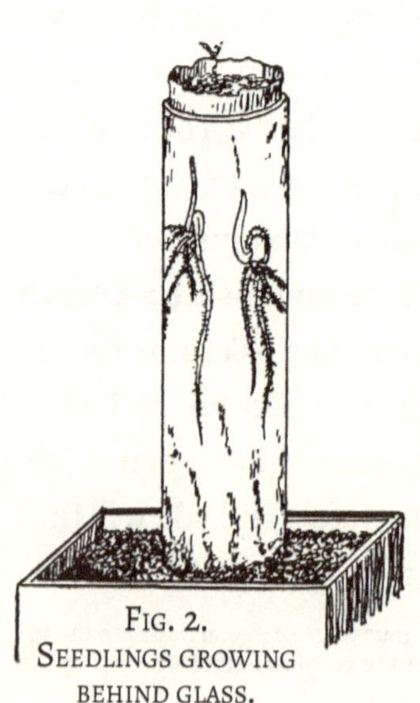

Fig. 2.
Seedlings Growing
Behind Glass.

sawdust. Place now the seeds between the paper and the glass; pushing them into position with a blunt wire. Put in the half of the French bean that has the plantlet attached to it. Fix, now, the glass tube in a pot or box of earth, and keep the earth and the sawdust moist. By this plan you can watch the seeds growing as easily as you can watch bees in a glass hive.

7. **The scar on the seed.** And now while we are waiting for the seed to grow, let us look again at a whole French bean. You notice the rounded back and that the opposite side is hollowed and has a scar. (See fig. 4.) If you have ever helped to shell beans or peas you will guess at once that the scar is the point where the bean was fixed to the pod.

8. **A seed with a large plantlet.** Examine also peas and broad beans and then split them open. In all these cases the plantlet is small, but if you will open a castor-oil seed, you will find a plantlet as long as the seed itself. Remove the beautiful mottled outer skin of the castor-oil seed, and then, with knife or fingernail, break the seed gently into its halves. If you have done this carefully, you will now see on one of the halves the stem, and above it the leaf of the plantlet. Stem and leaf together cover the whole space. Use now your lens and you will

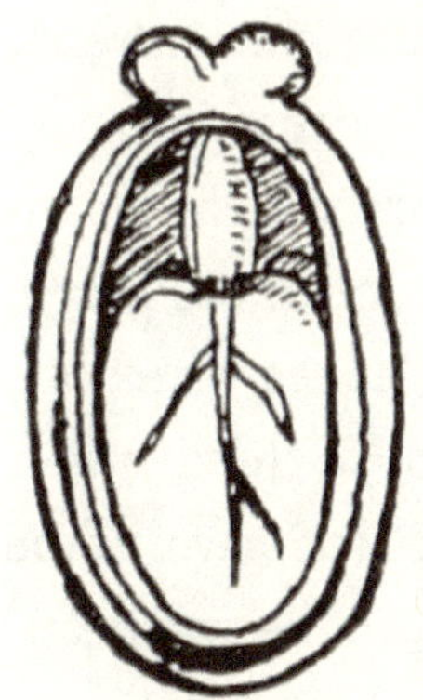

Fig. 3.
Castor-oil seed split
to show plantlet.

see distinctly the veining of the leaf. Note also the tiny leaf-ruff just above the stem. This is the first pair of true leaves of the castor-oil seedling.

9. **The little root in the seed.** Coming back to the split French bean, we must now look for the little root below the plantlet.

This root is so placed that it comes out of the seed-skin by a little door near the scar. Allow a whole bean to germinate, and you will see the tiny white root pushing through this little door close to the scar. As soon as the root is clear of the bean, it begins to point downwards.

10. **The seed-leaves.** Meantime the plantlet is growing larger. In a few days the leaves begin to take a green tint, and the green colour spreads to the stem just below the leaves, and to the whole of the bean-half. The root continues white. Already we can see that our guess was correct. The bean-half is one of the green, fleshy leaves which we saw above the ground, and the little leaves of the plantlet are the true leaves. And so, we shall call the two bean-halves that turn into green fleshy leaves—seed-leaves. We see now that the halves in split peas are just seed-leaves that have been pulled apart.

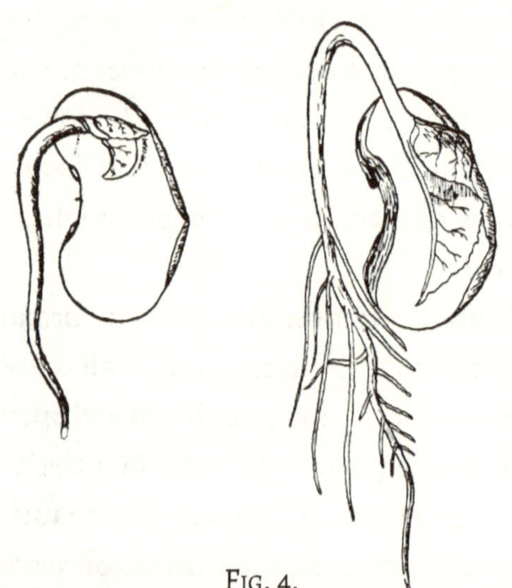

FIG. 4.

BEAN-HALF GROWING: ALL THE SEEDLING ABOVE THE TRUE ROOTS IS NOW BECOMING GREEN.

11. And now the green stem gets longer and longer, and takes the form of a loop above the bean-half. It is clear that the loop is trying to lift the seed-leaf into the air, and so you must press in the blotting-paper so that the seed-leaf can get out. If you do this, you will see, in a day or two, the loop lifting out the bean-

half which is now a green, fleshy leaf. We have now been able to watch every step from the swelling of the seed to the opening of the second pair of leaves—the first pair of true leaves.

12. **The three needs in germination.** We have seen that seeds need heat and moisture before they will grow. They also need air. Light is not needed, and indeed, seeds germinate faster when light is shut out.

<u>Exercises, experiments, etc.:</u>

(1) Most seeds germinate like the French bean, but the seed-leaves of some plants remain in the ground. Make experiments with the garden pea, broad bean, sunflower, pumpkin, acorn, castor-oil seed, cress.

*Notes.* – (a) In each experiment a scholar should be made responsible for watering, for marking dates, and so on. (b) Grow some sunflower seedlings in a pot to be ready for the experiment described in Chapter 9.

(2) Suspend an acorn over water by a piece of string in the neck of a wide-mouthed glass jar. If the weather be warm, the evaporating water will moisten the acorn and cause germination. To show that light is not necessary, a second jar could be placed in a dark place.

(3) As a boy was stooping over a barn floor, a mass of hay fell on his back. How could the boy exert most force to free himself? Compare the method of the French bean seedling in bursting through the ground.

(4) Some split peas were accidentally sown, and some came up. Explain how this could be.

**Composition exercise**: Tell the story of a French bean plant from the seed to the first pair of true leaves.

**Drawing exercise**: Draw a French bean, (a) dry, (b) germinating; showing the progress of growth at intervals. Mark the date on each sketch.

II.

# How Seeds Germinate

<u>PART II.</u>

1. **Seeds with one seed-leaf.** We have watched the germination of the French bean, a seed that has two seed-leaves. Most of our garden plants have two seed-leaves, but the grasses, lilies and some other plants have only one seed-leaf. Now, no garden plant is so important as the wheat plant—the queen of the grasses; and so we must look closely at the seed of wheat, and then watch how it germinates.

2. **What is inside a Wheat-seed.** Slice open a well-soaked wheat seed, using a sharp knife. The seed does not split into halves like the French bean, and so we must cut through. Cut downwards from the hairy end to the wrinkled end. The knife passes through white "flour," and lays bare the plantlet lying between the wrinkled end and the flour. The plantlet is a little disc of a dull white colour quite different from the white of the flour. This disc is the seed-leaf; and its business is to cover the plantlet and to feed on the flour. The true leaves cannot yet be seen, nor can the little root be seen. The flour is the food

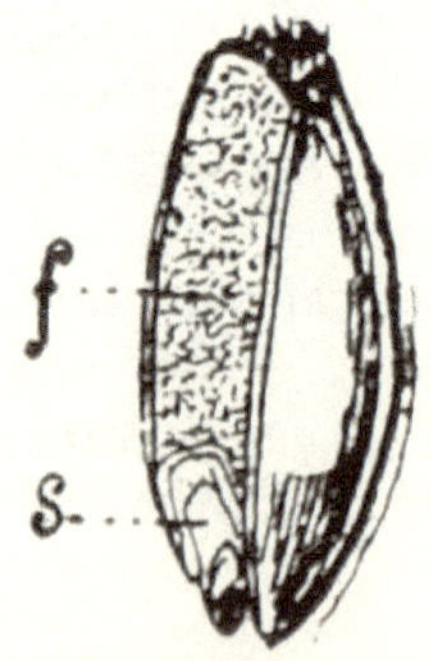


Fig. 5
WHEAT SEED CUT OPEN, TO SHOW THE FLOUR, THE SEED-LEAF.

that gives the young plant a start in life before it can gather food for itself. The flour is stored up to feed the seedling just as the white of an egg is stored up to feed a chicken.

3. **But here you say:** "There is no flour in the French bean; how then does the seedling get its food?" It feeds, I reply, on the thick seed-leaves. When you eat haricot beans you are taking the same kind of food as the French bean seedling. Split open an acorn, which is another seed that has no seed-flour. Note how small the plantlet is, and how great is the store of food in the two thick halves, and you will understand what a fine start the oak seedling gets in life. Take up the acorn after the seedling has grown for a time, and you will find that the plant has eaten all the food in the acorn halves. Test this also with a wheat plant.

4. **How a Wheat seed grows.** And now we can look at the wheat seedlings as they grow behind glass; and we shall compare them with the French bean seedling. A little white root is pushing its way out from the wrinkled end of one of the seeds. Next time we look, there are three roots, all coming from the wrinkled end, and a tiny green shoot has come out from the same place. Root and shoot have broken through the seed-leaf that sheathed them. In the French bean one root only came out from the seed; but in the wheat several roots come out. Another difference is that all of these wheat roots do not grow straight down like the first root of the French bean. Some of the roots grow sideways as well

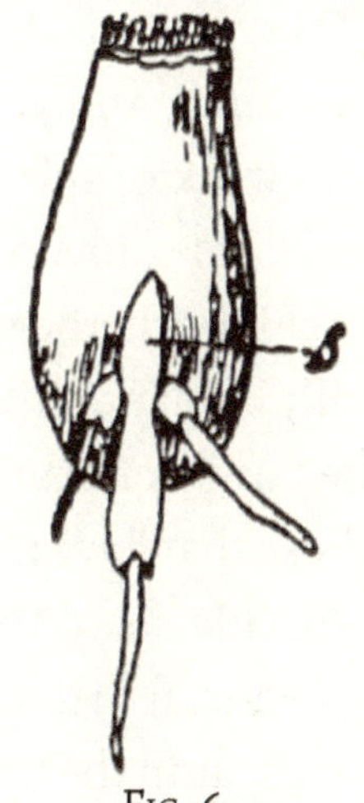

Fig. 6<br>Wheatseed germinating. The shoot (s) is green, and the three roots white

as downwards. Again, the main root of the French bean shows to the naked eye no hairs; but in the wheat roots the hairs are so many and so large that you can see them without your lens. But both in French bean and wheat the green shoot grows straight up.

5. When we next look, we find that the top of the wheat shoot is of a darker green than the lower part of the shoot. Use your lens and you will see that the lower part with the brownish-green is a sheath, and that the dark-green part is a new shoot that has broken out of this sheath. In a few days, this new shoot gives off a broad leaf, and, a little further up, another leaf.

6. **The veins in the leaves.** Take one of these wheat leaves and hold it to the light and you will see that the veins all run upwards, side by side. Take now a leaf—a true leaf, of the French bean, and you will see that there is a network of veins. Remember this difference carefully; for it is one of the ways of telling whether a plant belongs to the family of plants with two seed-leaves or to the family of plants with one seed-leaf. All those that have the veins running up side by side, as in the wheat leaf, have but one seed-leaf; all those that have a network of veins, as in the leaf of the French bean, have two seed-leaves.

7. **The Roots.** Coming back now to the roots, we notice that the stout main root

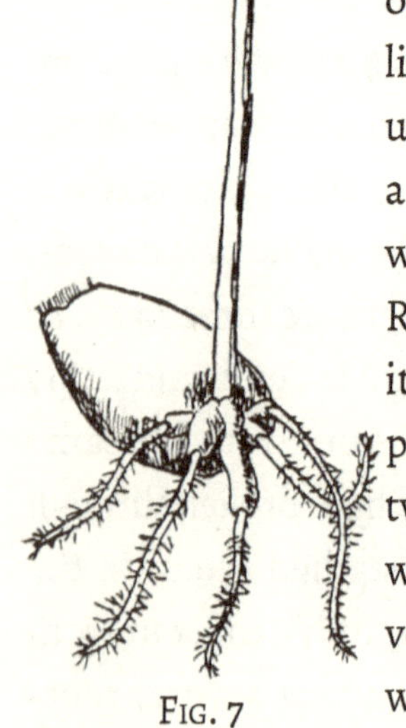

Fig. 7
Wheat seed germinating, showing the hairy roots and the second stage of the shoot. Compare with Fig. 4.

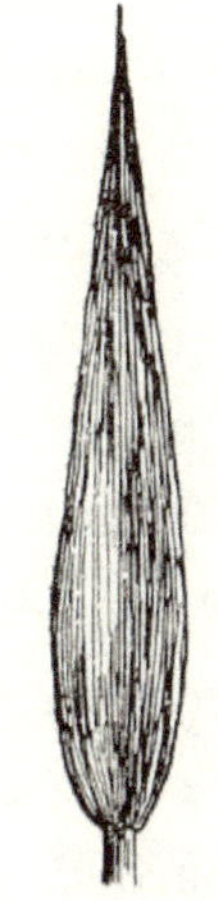

Fig. 8
LEAF OF A PLANT
WITH ONE
SEED-LEAF

of the French bean—the tap-root—has thrown out slender side-roots (fig. 4). The tap-root has grown quickly downwards to get out of reach of drought, and the side-roots have been thrown out to seek food, and to help to fix the seedling in case of storm. They act like the tent-ropes that fasten down a tent. Pull up one of the seedlings gently, and you will find that earth comes up with the roots. Even when you rinse the root, some earth remains. This is because the little hairs on the roots are sticky. In this way the roots get a firm hold of the earth. If you live near a river, you may have seen the roots of a tall gum tree laid bare. Where the bank is washed away you can often trace the great roots for an astonishing distance. Besides these great roots you now know that there are thousands of slender rootlets that cling to the soil. You wonder no longer that the tree stands firm in the storm.

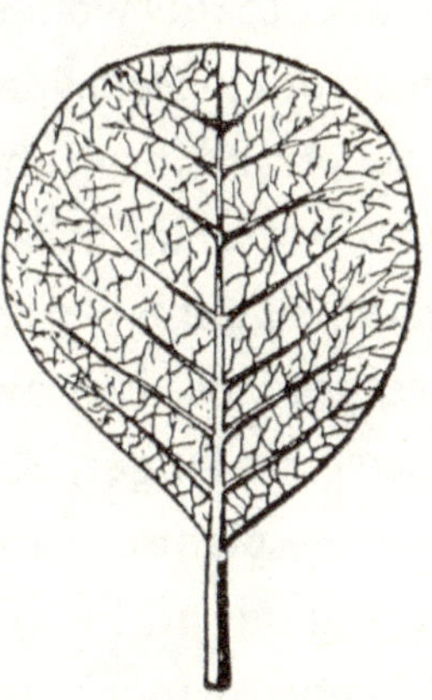

Fig. 9
LEAF OF A PLANT WITH
TWO SEED-LEAVES.

8. **The wonderful root-tip**. The tip of the root does its work so cleverly that it has been called the brain of the root. It chooses its path as if it had the powers of an insect groping its way with delicate "feelers." You must remember that this little delicate thread-like root cannot thrust the earth aside like a mole-cricket, or eat its way through the hard clods like the worm. It must find a way where there seems to be no way. It gets round an obstacle

or squeezes through close clods in a most wonderful manner. Again, if there is the slightest moisture, it moves towards it as if drawn by some magnet[4]. The point of the root would soon be worn off by all this wear and tear, but for a little cap that protects the tip. This root-cap is constantly being renewed; just as the point of a worn plough-share is renewed by the blacksmith. Of course there is no magic in this. The root cannot move towards the water till some of the moisture has reached the root-hairs.

9. **How the root behaves when the tip is lost**. The greatest danger to this wonderful root-tip comes, not from hard work, but from insects. Many insects, like the wire-worm, the mole-cricket, and the grub of the cockchafer, live as greedily on roots as a caterpillar lives on leaves. The root-tip is therefore often eaten; and it is a strange fact that when this happens the root seems to lose its way like an insect that has lost its "feelers." It may grow longer, but it does not, as before, move downwards. But the plant must have downward-roots; and so new roots spring out of the injured root and grow downwards. Shift a downward-root with a blunt wire so that it points sideways. In a little time, it will begin to point again downwards. Repeat the experiment, having first cut off the tip, and watch what happens. Have you ever noticed that when the top shoot of a pine tree is broken off, one or two of the side branches take up its work and grow upwards? Compare with this what happens to your injured root.

---

4      Of course there is no magic in this. The root cannot move towards the water till some of the moisture has reached the root-hairs.

<u>Experiments and Exercises.</u>

(1) Continue experiments on the seeds mentioned in the last chapter.

(2) Find an old tree that has thrown up suckers from the roots. Measure the distance from the stem to the furthest sucker, and compare with the height or reach of the tree. If the tree has "suckered" all round, you can, in this way, see the root-area.

*Note.*—Pears, white poplars, elms, and some plums often sucker freely.

(3) Compare the stem of a pine tree with the tap-root of a dandelion or of a mallow weed.

**Composition Exercise.**—Write an account of the root-tip and its work.

**Drawing Exercise.**— (1) Make drawings of a wheat seedling grown behind glass, at various stages, marking dates. (2) Draw side by side (*a*) a wheat leaf, (*b*) a French bean leaf, to show the different veining.

III.

# The Root

PART I.

1. **How the root feeds by drinking.** The great tree was hungry, and the little root far out from the trunk was searching for food in the hot, dry ground. Now, there was in the earth the very food that the tree needed. This food was close to the root, nay was touching it, and yet the root could not lay hold of it. The great tree was starving in the midst of food, because the earth was quite dry. The tree could not eat, because the little root could not drink.

2. A great thunderstorm came, and the warm rain soaked down to the earth, where the little root waited. The food in the earth passed into the water, and the root drank eagerly. Along the little root to the great root, and from the great root to the trunk, travelled the precious food. Then it climbed up the stem, and ran along the branches; it flowed into the twigs, and shoots, and spurs; it pushed into the leaves, and into every vein of the leaves; and soon the whole tree, from the tiniest root to the topmost leaf, was full of new life!

3. **The foods supplied to the tree by the root.** "But, do not the leaves feed the tree?" you ask. Yes, by far the greater part of a tree's food is got by the leaves; but the tree needs lime, iron,

and other foods that can only be got from the earth[5]. The tree needs only a very small amount of this root-food, but cannot live without it. If you tear off a fresh green leaf from a plant and put it in water, it will go on making food out of the air, but it has soon to stop and one reason is that it can no longer get any root-food; and, without this root-food, it cannot use the air-food.

The roots are not made for taking in solid food: they can take in fluids only; and, therefore, the food must be in a liquid form. This is one reason why the roots must have water. Another reason is that all the materials needed by the tree in its many parts are water-borne. And, so, without water, food-supplies are soon cut off.

4. **But now you exclaim**: "How can water climb up a great tree?" Yes, it is a wonderful piece of work. You will feel this if you carry a bucket of water up a long stair, and remember that a tree can quickly pull up many times this weight. Even a single sunflower can soon pull up a pailful of water.

5. **How can water climb up a tree?** Well, you must know that the root, like every other part of the plant, is built up of tiny cells (See Fig. 13). The root-hairs, too, are just long cells by which the root drinks. These hair-cells have very thin walls, so that the water gets easily through into the cell. But, when the water has got inside the cell, it cannot get out again; and when the cell gets so full that it can hold no more, it squeezes some water into the next. This cell in the same way gets too full, and squeezes some water into the third cell; and so on, up the root, and up the stem. Besides this root-pressure which **pushes** the water up the tree, there is another force that **pulls** the water up.

5     And nitrogen, phosphorus, potash, sulphur, &c.

This second force is caused by the evaporation of water through the leaves, and we shall hear more of it when we study the leaf.

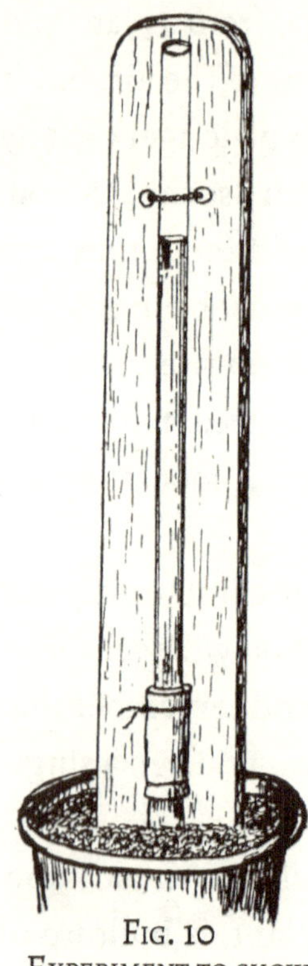

Fig. 10
Experiment to show
root-pressure.

6. **Two experiments to prove that the root lifts water.** How great the root-pressure is in spring you may see if you cut a grape-vine a little above the root. You will be astonished at the strong flow of sap. It flows and flows as if it would never stop. Looking at the rush of sap, you wonder no longer that a dry, dead-looking vine-stump can, in a few weeks, cover the side of a house with beautiful vine leaves. Cut also the stem of a young sunflower, or any of your seedlings that are growing strongly, and you will see a drop of water oozing out.

7. Another pretty experiment is the following: Take a young, strong garden balsam that is growing in a pot. Cut off the stem squarely, near the earth. Take a short piece of rubber tubing and slip it over the stem, and tie firmly. Then pour a little water into the tubing to keep the stump moist. Take now a piece of glass tubing, and fit it into the rubber tubing. Tie tightly, and then, in order to keep the glass-tubing upright, fix it to a stake. The water, in a few hours, will rise in the tube and continue to do so for a day or two. The soil must be watered as if the plant were uncut.

8. **How the water passes from the earth into the root.** And now I am ready for the question which you have been wait-

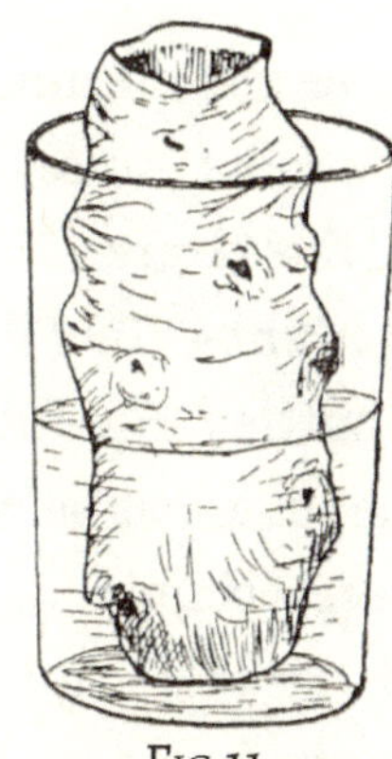

Fig. 11

TUBE MADE OF A POTATO, TO SHOW HOW ROOTS SUCK UP WATER.

ing to put: "How is it that the water passes from the earth into the root-cell, but cannot pass from the root-cell into the earth?" To understand this, take a large, long potato, and hollow it out carefully, as shewn in the figure. Place in the bottom of this potato-tube a dessert-spoonful of sugar, and then place the tube in a tumbler that has a little water in it. Mark on the tumbler the level of the water, and note how, in a day or two, this water is drawn into the tube and up the tube. In a few days the water may be at the brim of the potato-tube. And now reverse the process. Empty the potato-tube and tumbler, and put pure water in the potato, and strong sugared water in the tumbler. The water will now pass from the potato into the tumbler.

9. Now, what does all this mean? It means that the flow of liquid is always from the weaker to the stronger fluid. This is why the water, in both cases, flowed towards the sugared water. Now, the fluid in the root-cell is stronger than the fluid in the earth, and so the earth-fluid passes into the root-cell.

10. **Why does too much salt in a soil hurt plants?** Water the earth in a pot containing some of your sunflower seedlings with a strong solution of salt. The outside fluid is now the stronger; and so the fluid in the roots will pass out into the earth, and the seedlings will wilt. This will help you to see why most plants cannot grow in soils that contain much salt. At Mildura whole orchards have been ruined by soil containing too much salt. In good soils the fluid in the root-cells is always stronger than

Fig. 12
An imitation
plant-cell, after being
immersed in water.

the earth-fluid; and so there is nothing to check the flow into the roots. An easy experiment will make all this clearer.

11. **A make-believe plant-cell.** Fill a small wide-mouthed bottle quite full with water in which some sugar has been melted. From a clean sheep's bladder cut out a cover for the mouth. Tie this firmly, and place the whole bottle on its side in a vessel of water. In a day or two take it out, and note how the bladder-lid has bulged out. The strong fluid inside the bottle has sucked in some of the weaker fluid. Place now the bottle in a vessel containing a very strong sugar-fluid; using more sugar than will melt. This causes fluid to pass from the sugar-fluid inside to the stronger sugar-fluid outside, and the bladder-lid no longer bulges. Now, if instead of a bottle with a bladder-lid, we could try a root-cell, we should see it behaving in the same way. When you remember that each root-hair is one little cell, and that the plant-root, stem, leaves, and flowers—is built up entirely of small cells, you will see the importance of the experiments we have just been making.

12. **What becomes of the fluid-foods received by the root?** If you melt salt in water, and then leave this water in the sun, the water will disappear into the air and the salt remain. In the same way, most of the fluid taken in by the roots passes into the air through the leaves but the mineral food remains in the tree. Sometimes a mineral that is not good for the plant finds

its way in this manner into the leaves; but when the leaves fall the plant gets rid of these harmful or useless minerals.

<u>Exercises and Out-door Work:</u>

(1) The sap gets thicker as it goes up a tree, owing to the escape of water by evaporation from the leaves. Show how this helps to lift the water from the roots to the leaves.

(2) Seek opportunities of seeing how deep roots go. Railway cuttings and other excavations offer chances of study. In dry districts a tiny plant may have a root 20 inches long. Summer annuals especially have to make haste to tap the moisture which is beyond the reach of drought. Dig up carefully some summer weeds, and examine the roots.

**Composition Exercise:** Tell how a plant drinks through its roots, and how the fluid is lifted up to the leaves.

**Drawing Exercise:** Take up carefully a seedling. Try to get all the roots spread out as they were in the earth, and make a drawing.

IV.

# The Root

<u>PART II</u>

1. **What the root seeks and avoids.** The first use of a root is to fix the young plant in the soil; and the second use is to seek food in the soil. And so it has come to pass that the tiny white root points downwards from the very first, just as the tiny green shoot strives upwards from the very first. The root therefore has learned to shun the light, just as the green shoot has learned to seek the light. We can see how strong is this habit from the air roots of the ivy. Examine these roots, and you will find that they always grow away from the light and on the shady side of the stem. We can see how hard the root tries to escape the light in roots like that of the carrot, that actually shrink into the soil. Look also at the tip of a bramble shoot that has rooted, and you will see how strongly the root pulls the tip into the earth.

2. **Why does the root keep near the surface?** But here you ask: "Since the root goes down, why does it not go farther down?" Well, there are several reasons. One is that the moisture comes from rain or dew that may not sink far. Another reason is that the deep soil may be too cold. A third reason is that the soil near the surface is better aired. A root, like a germinating seed, needs warmth and air as well as moisture. Trees sometimes,

in hot weather, send their roots too far down into cold sodden sub-soil. Such trees suffer from wet feet." The monks of old knew this, and would place a large flat stone under the roots of their peaches to keep them from going into a cold subsoil. Also, the surface soil is richer in plant food, and so the roots run sideways as well as downwards.

3. **How roots and branches correspond.** Can you tell me now why the feeding roots of a tree are most numerous at the points where the rain runs off the leaves? In a shower, you sometimes stand under a tree as you would stand under a great umbrella. Watch where the rain drops as it runs off the leaves. If you dig at these points, you will find that the tree has placed feeding roots just where the rain drops. But there is no hard and fast rule; for the roots go on farther if there be good moist soil beyond. Often a root will run out in this way until it is longer than the highest point of the tree.

4. **How sodden ground hurts the root.** The root must have moisture, but too much moisture is almost as dangerous as too little. When there is too much moisture, the root cannot get air. An exploring root will avoid a sodden patch just as it will avoid a stone. A simple experiment will show the damage done to a plant by earth that is too wet. Place side by side in the open air, where they can get the rain, a well-drained pot of wheat seedlings and a jam-tin pot of wheat seedlings; both sown at the same time. Give exactly the same amount of water to each pot. The earthenware pot is porous to air, and any surplus water passes out at the side or through the hole in the bottom. The jam-tin cannot receive air through its sides, nor can it get rid of water when there is too much. Compare the growth of the

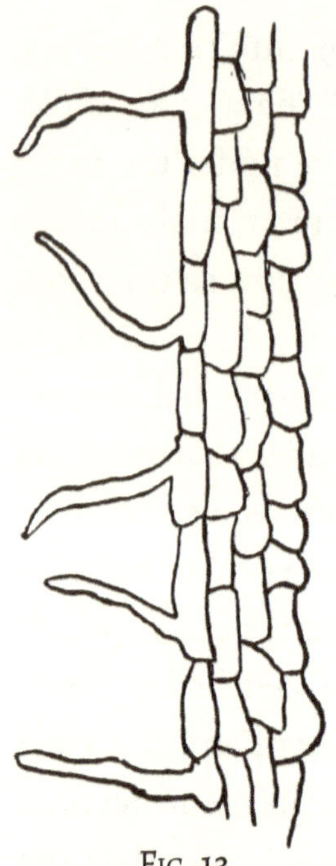

Fig. 13

Outer skin of root becoming wrinkled (much enlarged). Below this the hairs are simply extensions of cells.

seedlings in the pot and in the tin. When the wheat is about eight inches out of the ground, take the plants up carefully and look with a lens at the roots. On the well-drained roots you will find hundreds of tiny feeding hairs, while on the badly-drained roots these feeding hairs will be absent or few in number. No wonder the wheat in a wet patch of ground has a starved look.

5. **How the hairs on the root take in food.** The hairs on the root are, as we saw, delicate cells that suck in water. Now these hairs will not grow in soil that is kept constantly wet. Hence the poor growth of wheat in wet, badly-drained soil. In warm, loose, moist soil, on the other hand, the number of roots and rootlets and root-hairs is astonishing. Every particle of soil seems to be searched. A large marrow, growing in such soil, was found to have roots which, if put end to end, would have measured over 15 miles.

6. **Plants that thrive in wet ground.** But here you ask me: "Why, then, do some plants thrive in sodden ground, and even in water?" Well, you must never forget that Nature has no vacant plots in her great Earth-garden. Every patch of ground is turned to account to support life of some kind. And so plants have been gradually trained for wet soils and for ponds. You may see on the margin of a pond a grass, or reed, or tree that

likes to have its roots always in sodden soil. Further in, you find a plant that likes to have its feet in water and its stem in the air; and, still further in, you see a plant that likes to have both stem and root in water.

7. If the water were always at the same level, the plants best suited for each place would always be found in that place; but since the water level often changes, there is a constant struggle between the various kinds of plants to get the soil that suits them. Those that are half of the water and half of the land will march in towards the water in years of drought; but are driven back to the bank when the water rises again. In times not yet long past, great parts of the earth were marshy and undrained; and therefore we need not wonder that so many plants are at home in water or in sodden ground. But nearly all the higher plants and nearly all the plants of use to man, need well-drained soil, loose and open to the air.

<u>Problems and Exercises:</u>

(1) Place a seedling, grown in a pot, on its side, in order to show that the green shoot persists in growing upwards.

(2) In studying the downward pull of roots, examine the runners of strawberries and the wrinkles in a parsnip root.

(3) In the carrot, rhubarb, and dock, note that the leaves are arranged so as to drain the rain and dew towards the centre. Shew how the root plan corresponds.

(4) It is often useless in watering an old tree to throw water at the foot of the stem. Give the reason.

(5) When a gardener, in taking up a tree, loses half the roots, why must he also cut back the branches to the same extent?

(6) Explain why well-drained land yields much larger and finer crops than undrained land. Describe the appearance of wheat plants on low, wet parts of the field.

(7) The willow is sometimes planted in damp, undrained soil to help to keep the ground dry. Explain how some trees can thrive in soil like this.

**Composition Exercise:** Tell the adventures of a root as it travels in search of root-food.

**Drawing Exercise:** Make a drawing of a tree whose branches hang umbrella-like over the earth; and shew by faint lines below the surface where the feeding roots are placed.

# V

# The Root

## PART III

1. We must now look at a number of roots of different plants, and try to find out the various root-plans.

2. **Tap-roots and Fibrous roots.** In plants like the dandelion, we find a distinct tap-root and many small side-roots. This tap-root is just the first root become large. It has grown straight

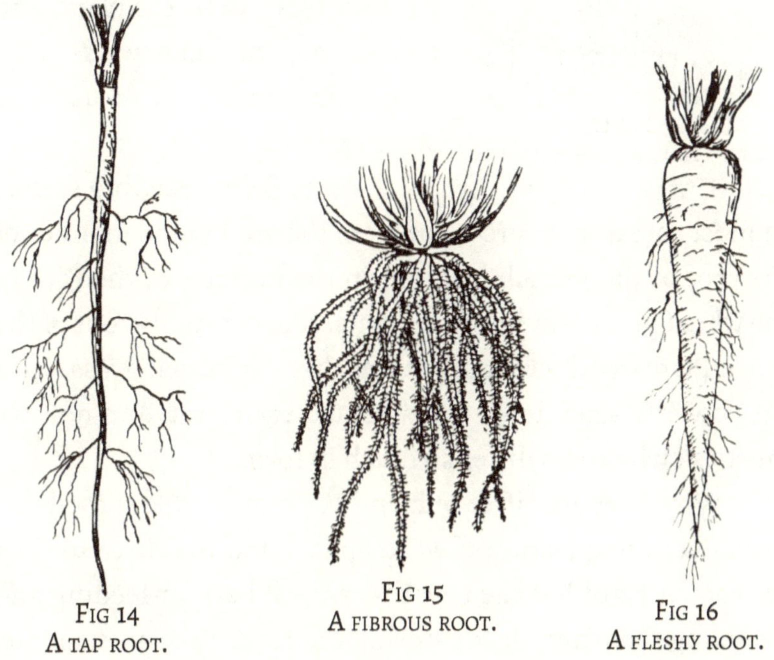

FIG 14
A TAP ROOT.

FIG 15
A FIBROUS ROOT.

FIG 16
A FLESHY ROOT.

down and grown much thicker than any of the side-roots. In many plants the tap-root is not so clearly seen as in the dandelion, and in some roots, indeed, you cannot find a tap-root at all. Where all the roots or many of the roots are slender, as in the wheat plant, the root is called a **fibrous root.**

FIG 17
ROOTS FROM A CREEPING STEM
(AFTER VON MUELLER).

3. **Fleshy roots**. Other plants, again, like the carrot, have fleshy roots. These fleshy roots are just underground stores of food for the plant. Sometimes the food is stored in one mass, as in the carrot; sometimes the store is spread over several fleshy roots, as in the dahlia. We have seen that every root has two uses – to fix the plant, and to seek food. And now we see that some roots have a third use – to store up food.

4. **Roots from creeping stems.** In most cases, roots grow out from the seed in the manner of the root of the French bean, or in the manner of the root of the wheat plant. But in some plants, roots grow also out of the stem. Plants with **creeping stems**, like the couch grass, have the power to send down a new root at each knot. And now we must ask why roots differ so much in form.

5. **Why do roots differ in form?** We may be able sometimes to answer the question if we keep in mind the three uses of the root. A plant has the root that suits it best for feeding and for fixing the plant, or for storing the food. Take an example.

Why has the carrot a fleshy root? Because the carrot's plan of life is this: The first year it gives up its whole time to growing green leaves and storing up food. Everything that it can save it puts into the root, which is a kind of plant savings bank. Then, in the second year, it uses this store of food to make flowers and seeds. If you examine the carrot root after the seeds have ripened, you will find that the store of food is gone. In the same way, you expect to find in a plant that has lived for ages in a very dry land a deep root or a swollen root – a root formed to live through drought.

6. But now comes a question I have been expecting: "Do not the roots eat up all the food in the soil; and what do they do then?" Nature meets this difficulty in several ways. One way is to supply fresh food, and another is to remove the plant to a fresh piece of ground.

7. **How Nature renews the root-foods.** When a wheat plant has grown up, man cuts it down and carries it off. With every waggon of wheat that leaves a field, a part of the root-food of that field is lost; but when grass grows wild it dies down and returns to the soil the food that it got from it. Trees strew the ground beneath them with leaves and bark and twigs, all of which, when decayed, make root-food. Then, again, millions of creatures die every season and enrich the earth. An animal lives on plants; and therefore, when it dies, becomes food for the plants. While the animal is alive, its droppings help to renew the root-foods. The burying-beetle that covers up these droppings with soil is a most useful food-getter for the roots.

8. **How the good farmer imitates Nature.** The good farmer imitates Nature's plans as closely as he can. He returns to the

field all the straw and all the animal droppings that he can collect. He even imitates the burying-beetle; for he covers the manure with soil, and thus prevents the sun from drying it up. He sends to lonely islands where bird-droppings have accumulated for ages, and brings home the guano for his fields. He buys bones from the butcher, and grinds them into dust, and scatters the bone-dust on his ground.

9. **How Nature seeks fresh soil for her plants.** But Nature has another plan for getting fresh food for the roots: she moves the plants from time to time. Sometimes, as in the case of a travelling bulb, she moves the plant a little way every year; at other times, as in the case of the thistle, the new plant springs up from seed that has travelled a great way. Then there are the creeping-stem plants that root at the joints. When the old root dies, the new roots, in fresh soil, are able to continue the plant's life. Make experiments with couch grass, buffalo grass, or with the runners of the strawberry plant, and you will see this for yourself. Watch, too, the suckers thrown up by the roots of a poplar, an elm, or a pear tree. In all these cases, Nature is sucking fresh soil for her plants.

FIG 18

NEW BULB FORMING AT THE SIDE OF THE OLD BULB.

10. Again, if you dig up all the plants in a piece of ground that has never been touched by man, you will find that some of the roots are surface-feeders, and that others go deep. In this way, all the root-food, shallow and deep, is made use of. Even

when the roots of two plants seem to be feeding at the same level on the same soil, the one plant may be using one kind of food and the other plant a different kind. Roots, therefore, that seem crowded may not really be crowded.

11. **How the good farmer imitates Nature: the rotation of crops.** In all this, the good farmer imitates Nature. He is ever planning to get fresh food for his crops. Last year, the forty-acre paddock was sown with turnips. Now the turnip has a short root, and therefore is a surface-feeder. Also, the turnip root takes a great deal of lime out of the soil. This year, the same paddock is sown with barley, which needs very little lime; and next year, it will be laid down in clover, which sends its roots deep into the ground. And so on, till the ground is ready for the turnips again; and the circle is complete. When a wheel circles round, it is said to rotate. Hence this plan of the farmer is called the **rotation of crops**. No man, you see, can be a good farmer who does not know what kind of food a plant needs, and whether it roots deep or near the surface. Nor can he be called a good farmer unless he stirs his ground deeply so that the roots may be able to go deep down for food and moisture.

12. **How the farmer can double his farm.** A farmer who farms in this way can make two blades to grow where one grew before; and this is as good as doubling the size of his farm. If all our farmers did this, it would be as good as doubling Victoria. The farmer who farms in this way will soon hold as high a place among men as the doctor or the lawyer or any other learned man. Such a farmer, too, will always be finding out something new; for there is much still to learn about plants and soils, and about the wonderful thing we call **life**. It was only the other day

that it was discovered that the roots need the help of minute creatures that live in the soil!

13. **How invisible creatures (Bacteria) work for the roots**. These earth-germs make the soil fit for root food. They are much too small to be seen by the naked eye. And not only are there tiny creatures in the soil to help the roots, but in some plants, if not in all, there are minute creatures in the roots themselves. If you look at the root of clover or scarlet runner or lupin or other plants of the same family, you will find little knots or swellings. These knots are made by masses of tiny living creatures that help the root to get food out of the air.[6]

14. **Real earth-fairies**. Not very long ago, people believed in earth-fairies that helped the plants to grow. Well, these earth-germs are the real fairies, and, in tending your little plot of ground, you must see that they are kept comfortable. The earth-germs need air. Now, if the surface of the earth be hard and caked, the air cannot easily get in. You must therefore keep the surface soil loose, so that the air may get easily in. Too much water in the soil also prevents the air from getting in, and therefore you must see that your plot is well-drained so that water may not lie in the soil but run through the soil. Never allow your plot to become sodden. Another way of keeping the earth in your plot well-aired is to use plenty of stable-manure; and this also provides food for the earth-germs. There are far more earth-germs in garden soil than in unbroken land, because in the garden the earth is kept loose and rich and well-drained.

6    The food got from the air by plants of the pea flower family (legumes) is nitrogen. The swelling on the roots are now dried and examined by chemists, and the dust sown in a particular way. This gives a crop of millions of the germs that cause the knots. Parcels of the germs are now sold in Europe and America to farmers whose soils are poor in these germs. This may turn out to be one of the greatest discoveries of the nineteenth century.

## Exercises and Out-door Work

(1)   What kind of roots have radish, chickweed, daffodil, turnip, corn, periwinkle, dock, violet?

(2)   Name any plants with (*a*) tap-root (*b*) fibrous roots (*c*) fleshy roots.

(3)   Name any root-stores that we use as food.

(4)   Explain how buffalo-grass travels and why it travels. Compare the garden violet (or the native ivy-leaved violet), couch grass, Danubian Reed ("bamboo").

(5)   Clear and loosen the ground below a joint in buffalo or couch grass, and note how long it takes to root.

(6)   Find out from the best farmers of your district examples of the rotation of crops.

(7)   Are the following wild flowers annuals or perennials[7]; and what kind of roots have they? The purple fringe lilies, the Australian blue bell, the harbinger of spring, cape weed, the Victorian crocus, the Bathurst burr, sundew.

(8)   When a farmer talks of a field being wheat-sick, what does he mean?

**Composition Exercise**. A carrot lives for two seasons: tell, in two chapters, the story of a carrot's life.

**Drawing Exercises.** (*a*) Draw a strawberry plant that is sending out runners to form new plants. (*b*) Draw a creeping stem rooting at the joints.

*Note*. Indicate the roots by faint lines.

---

7     See Chap. XXVII for annuals and perennials.

VI.

# The Stem

<u>PART I</u>

1. It is rare to find a boy in England who can handle an axe, but nearly every Australian boy knows how to make the chips fly. But not every boy can read the story of the wood he is chopping. And yet it is a wonderful story. One man looks at a great gum tree that has fallen to the axe and says: "It will burn well;" another says: "It will split into good palings;" a third: "It will make good railway sleepers;" and then comes a man who looks at the rings of the tree and says: "Here is the diary that the tree kept. It has been keeping this story of its life for a thousand years. Look" – and here he points to a place where the rings are all close together, "that was a time of drought when the tree made little growth; and here, where the rings are wide, is a time of good years when the sap ran free. For ten centuries the 'keets have come to its honey-pots in the time of flower; magpies and crows innumerable have perched on its branches, and thirty generations of First Australians have climbed up to the nest of the opossum." Who would not learn to read a story like this?

2. First, then, let us ask, **What has the stem of a plant to do?** It has two things to do: to hold the leaves and flowers up in the

44

air, and to act as a channel for the sap. First of all, we are to see how the stem holds the leaves and flowers up in the air.

3. **The stem as a leaf-supporter.** If you try to count the leaves on a great tree you will soon stop: there are so many. It must be a stout stem that can carry all these leaves. And each year there are more leaves, and the stem must become stronger. And so the stem gets thicker and thicker as the leaves grow more and more, until you cannot put your arms round the stem. And, as the tree grows older, all the middle part of the stem – **the heart-wood** – becomes dead and hard. It is this hard, dead heartwood that enables the tree to hold up its great mass of leaves and to face the storm. Look at a great gum tree in a strong wind. The young saplings near it that have as yet no heartwood bend almost to the ground; but the old gum tree bends not at all. Not for a thousand years has the old gum tree bent to the wind.

4. **Where the new stem-wood is placed.** Can you guess where the tree puts the new wood it makes during the growing season? In the middle? No, we have seen that the middle becomes dead and hard. Where then? On the outside of the old wood, and just below the bark. The living, active wood in a tree is to be found close to the bark.

5. **The bark.** And the bark – does it also put the new bark on the outside? No: you can see that the bark must put its new growth on the inside, because the outside gets old and cracked, and often, indeed, splits or peels off.[8] The bark is sometimes very elastic, and is able to stretch without breaking as the stem grows, but in most trees it splits or peels. In the elm it breaks

8     The thin formative layer which, on one side, makes the new wood, and on the other side, makes the new bark, is called the cambium (cambio, I change).

into ridges, and in the stringy-bark gum it peels off. The outer bark may be very thick, as in the cork oak or the stringy-bark gum, or it may be thin, as in the lemon-scented gum tree or the plane tree. As this bark peels off, fresh bark forms, and the tree is not hurt. Indeed, the tree is often healthier for losing this bark. The plane tree is able, in this way, to throw off the dust that gathers on the stem in summer; and this is one reason why it is so good a tree for our dusty streets.

6. Sometimes, as in a young wattle or lemon-scented gum, the outer bark is so thin that a scratch of the fingernail shows the **green layer** of the bark. Most trees, however, have a thick, dead outer bark to protect the tender growing new bark and new wood. You can now see that the living part of a tree – the new bark and new wood – lies between dead bark and dead wood. You will now understand how, by ringing, we can kill a tree without cutting the tree right through. All that we have to do is to cut through the bark to the new wood. You will understand also how it is that after a bush fire many of the trees are able, in a short time, to throw out new shoots. The living part of the tree was protected by the outer dead bark, and so new shoots can be made from the tree's reserve stores. Our "bush" trees, you see, have to lay up stores, not for a rainy day, but for a day of fire. Many of you have seen, within a few weeks of the fire, a beautiful fringe of green running along the blackened branches.

7. **A one-year old stem.** And now you are ready to see for yourself how wood and bark grow. Take a one-year old shoot of any quick-growing wood like the banksian rose, and make a slanting cut with a sharp knife. In the centre you have the soft pith (fig. 20 (1)), outside of the pith a ring of wood; and, outside of all,

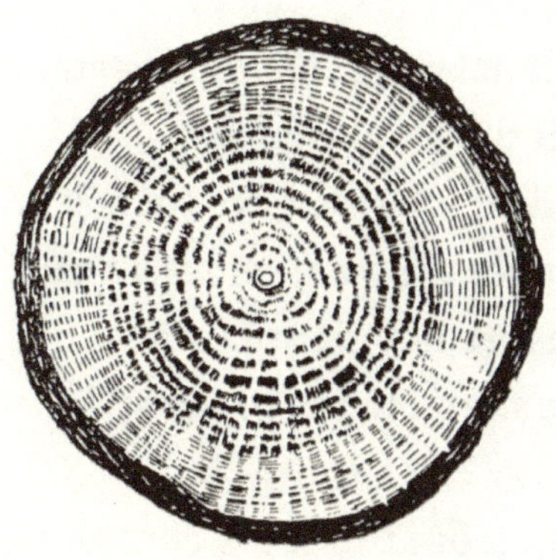

FIG 19

CUT STEM OF ACER TO SHOW THE ANNUAL RINGS. THE DARK WOOD (SAP-WOOD) HAS BEEN CUT AWAY. THE RAYS RUNNING FROM PITH TO BARK FORM BELOW THE WOOD.

the bark. On the outside of the bark you find a thin skin which afterwards thickens; below this there is the **green layer** of the bark, and still farther in we have the **inner bark.**

**A two-year old stem.** Take now a two-year old stem, and you will see (1) the pith, (2) the wood of the first year, (3) the new wood, (4) the bark. A three-year old stem will show (1) the pith, (2) the wood of the first year, (3) the wood of the second year, (4) the new wood, and (5) the bark. You can see now how the age

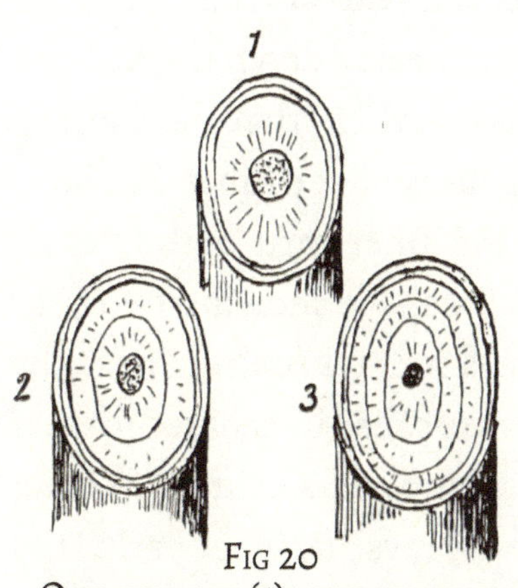

FIG 20

ONE-YEAR OLD (1), TWO-YEAR OLD (2), AND THREE-YEAR OLD (3) SHOOTS. IN NO. 2 THE FIRST RING OF WOOD IS DARK, AND THE THIRD RING OF WOOD, COUNTING FROM THE PITH. 3, THE SAP-WOOD (NEW WOOD.)

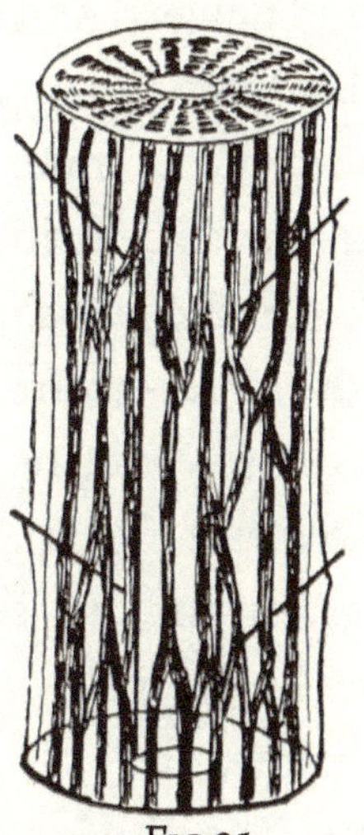

FIG 21

ONE-YEAR OLD CUTTING THE PITH AND THE PITH-RAYS OF THE WOOD.

of a tree can be told from these annual rings. Examine a stem of several years' growth, and count the annual rings[9].

8. **The stem as a sap-channel.** And now we have to look at the second duty of the stem. How does the stem serve as a sap-channel? And, first of all, you must remember that there are two kinds of sap to be carried – the sap from the roots, and the sap from the leaves.

9. **Root-sap tubes**. The raw sap from the roots comes up through tubes in the new wood; and so we shall call the new wood the **sap-wood**, to distinguish it from the hard old **heart-wood**. The root-sap runs up the tubes in the sap-wood to be mixed with the food gathered by the leaves from the air. Out of this mixture is made the ripe sap, which carries to the root the power to make new roots, to the wood the power to make new wood, and to the buds the power to make new shoots and leaves and flowers. And where does this **leaf-sap** find channels?

10. **Leaf-sap tubes**. The tubes that carry down the leaf-sap are placed in the inner bark. You see, then, that the leaf-sap tubes are not so deep in the tree as the root-sap tubes. But how, you ask, can the leaf-sap get into the inner parts of the stem?

11. **The silver-grain**. Take the cut shoot showing two-year old wood. Use your lens, and you will see rays running from the bark to the pith (fig. 21). These rays are called by cabinet-makers **silver-grain**, and they serve to carry the leaf-sap inwards from the inner bark. You will notice that the rays pierce the bark. They run right inwards to the pith, and are therefore sometimes called **pith-rays**. The **pith** is a storehouse of food for young shoots. It

9    In one growing season there may be a ring for the spring growth, and another ring for the summer growth, making two rings or layers in all. Several rings produced in one season are easily seen in the beech.

is very active in a one-year old plant; but, as the plant becomes older, the pith becomes smaller and less active, and finally dies and disappears.

Questions and Exercises:

A hide-bound tree is one in which growth is checked by unhealthy bark that cannot expand. Explain.

Can you see from the last question why it is important to grow trees so that the stems and branches are not bare to the sun?

Explain how ringing kills a tree.

**Composition Exercise**. Tell the story of how a tree was able at last to hold up thousands of leaves.

**Drawing Exercise**. Draw the cut stem of a tree that has leaves with a network of veins. Show the rings of annual growth.

*Note:* Two- or three-year old wood from a vigorous plum tree shows the rings well.

VII.

# The Stem

PART II

1. **Root-sap tubes and leaf-sap tubes.** We have seen that there are two kinds of sap-tubes, one kind running up from the root, and the other kind running down from the leaves. Perhaps you have heard of the wizard who could see the two streams of sap running side by side – one up and the other down! What wonders we could see inside a tree if we had eyes like his! And what sounds we could hear if only our ears were quicker! With quicker ears, the October woods would be filled with the noise of the rush of the spring-sap, sounding like the noise of many waters. It would be deafening; and it is well for us that our ears are dull!

2. You see, then, that just as the hard bones support the body of a man, so the **heartwood** supports the tree; and just as the veins carry the blood through the human body, so the sap-tubes carry the sap to all parts of the tree. And you must notice that the sap-tubes have very tough sides and so are able not only to carry sap to and from the leaves, but to support the stem and the leaves. The tubes that run into a leaf are thus able to act as bones as well as veins. And now we shall make...

3. **Experiments to show the water-path in stem and leaf.** Cut

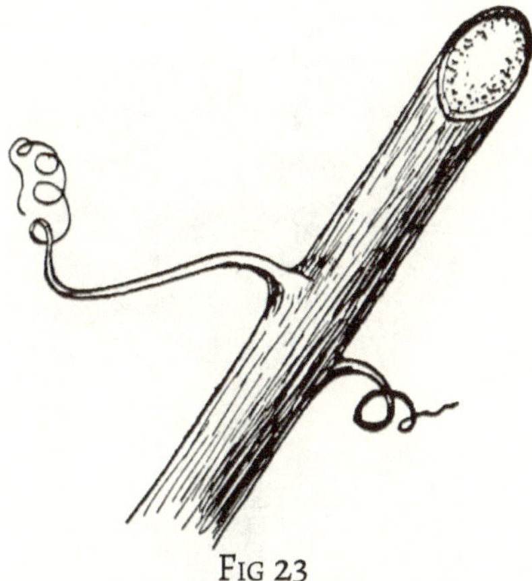

Fig 23

GRAPE VINE SHOOT. THE RING OF
DOTS BETWEEN PITH AND BARK
SHOWS THE ROOT-SAP TUBES.

a vine-shoot which ends in a leaf, and place the cut end in a vessel containing red ink. In a short time, you will see the red ink colouring the smallest veins. Then cut through the shoot with a sloping cut, and you will see a ring of small, red, round spots, showing the tubes up which the ink has flowed. This ring of red spots is between the bark and the pith. Since neither pith nor bark are red, we know that the ink has not run up the bark nor the pith[10]. Then split the shoot, and you will see the long red streaks that show where the ink has run. These red streaks are the tough tubes that run up from the smallest root-hairs to the smallest veins in the leaves. If you take a ring of bark off the stem of a growing plant you will not touch these tubes, and therefore the leaves will still receive water from the roots, and will not droop.

4. Cut, now, the leaf stalk of the vine near the point where it joins the stem, and note the tough tubes that run from the sap-wood into the leaf[11]. You can see how these tubes serve the leaf both as veins and bones. The stem too is strengthened by the ring of tough tubes, so that, long before the hard heartwood is formed, the tender-looking stem can stand the strain of a

---

10     Besides this quick movement up the sap-wood tubes there is a slower movement which, in time, stains the whole of the wood.

11     The ring of sap-tubes running up from the stem to the leaf-stalk can be seen very clearly on the leaf scar of the Virginia creeper.

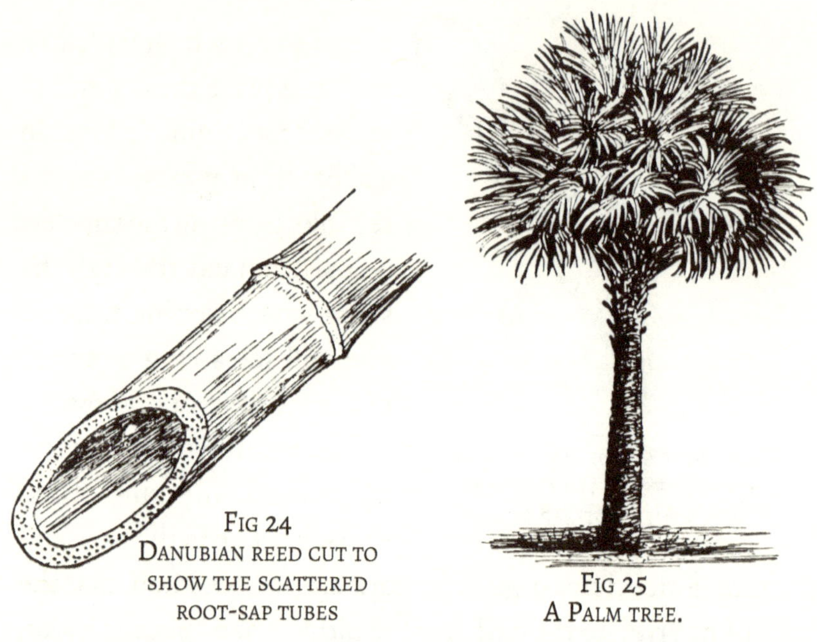

FIG 24
DANUBIAN REED CUT TO
SHOW THE SCATTERED
ROOT-SAP TUBES

FIG 25
A PALM TREE.

storm in a way that fills an architect with wonder and delight. Look at a daffodil bending to a spring breeze; look at a field of wheat swaying with graceful ease as gust follows gust, and you may have some faint idea of what passes through the mind of an architect who studies Nature.

5. **The water path in plants that have one seed-leaf.** Cut a shoot of the Danubian reed—often called "bamboo" (fig. 24)— and place the cut end in the red ink as before. Note that the reed has a hollow centre instead of pith. In a short time, you will find the red spots as before, but this time, not in a ring inside the bark, but scattered all over the solid part of the stem. Note carefully that this is the plan for sap-tubes in all reeds, grasses, lilies, palms, and other plants that have the veins running side by side—the plants that have only one seed-leaf. In all plants

that have the veins in a network—the plants that have two seed-leaves—we have the root-sap tubes placed as in the vine-shoot.

6. **How palms and reeds grow.** Note, too, that palms and other trees of that class do not grow by adding an annual ring of wood outside the old wood. The new growth is added at the top, and so the stem is nearly of the same thickness at the top as at the bottom. Each year a new bunch of leaves is produced at the top, while the leaves of previous years gradually wither and fall.

7. Just as the age of an oak tree can be guessed from the rings in the stem, so the age of a palm can often be guessed from the number of rings of leaf-scars on the stem. When the stem is smooth, as in tropical palms, the rings can be counted very easily, but it is less easy with some of the palms of colder lands because the stems may be covered with a thick warm coating of fibre to protect the tree from frost[12].

8. **How a tree ringed halfway round behaves.** You will now be able to see how it is that a tree may live for a long time after it has lost its heartwood and become hollow. You will also be able to see how it is that a tree may live on, after part of the bark has been removed. The tree dies, of course, if the bark is removed all round the tree; but if even a narrow path be left for the sap-tubes, the tree can often keep some of the branches in healthy leaf. On the footpath that runs beside the railway line from Jolimont to Richmond, there is a gum tree bearing this inscription: "A bark canoe was cut from this tree by the wild blacks prior to the arrival of the white man." At the top and

12      A tropical palm can be seen in the Palm House of the Melbourne Botanic Gardens, and its palmate leaves are many fine palms of a hardier kind.

bottom, the marks of the stone tomahawk are still visible. The bark that was left was sufficient to keep the tree alive, and it bears leaves to this day. The rush of healing sap has made the edges of the wound fold over in the usual way. You can see how those edges reached out in the vain attempt to bridge over the gap and how they finally fell back on the living part of the tree, leaving the hard, dead heartwood exposed to the air. It is probably more than a century since this happened; and today the hard dead heartwood looks as little a part of the tree as if it were a great stake of dead wood fixed for the support of the part that is still alive.

### Questions and Exercises:

(1) To show the water-path in the stem, make experiments with garden balsam, geranium, and bleached celery.

*Note:* In the balsam the red sap-tubes can be seen through the thin bark.

(2) How is it that a hollow tree may stand for many years if only it has strength enough to stand against the wind?

(3) Look in the annual rings of an old tree for the old root-sap tubes—no longer used. The tubes look like pores.

(4) The hollow stem in wheat plant or reed is stronger than a solid stem would be. Has man taken the hint in any of his building plans?

(5) Give examples of plants that have burrowing stems.

(6) Give examples of trees that are conical in shape (pine) and spreading (elm).

**Composition Exercise.** Tell how the water runs up and down a stem.

**Drawing Exercise.** Draw an old stem to show the annual rings.

Draw cut shoots of (*a*) vine, (*b*) Danubian reed, to show the water-paths. Use colour to show the sap-tubes.

VIII.

# Climbing Plants and Parasites

1. Every plant tries to get up into the light. If it could whisper its wish in your ear, you would hear it say: "How can I get my leaves up and up into the air and sunshine?" And each plant has its own way of climbing up. One, like the gum tree, makes itself so hard and strong that it can hold ten thousand leaves up in the air; another, like the ivy, climbs nearly as high, but only with the help of the gum tree; a third, like the mistletoe, perches on a high branch and sucks its juices; and a fourth, like the dodder, lives entirely on the plant round which it winds. Nay, there are beautiful climbing orchids in the Queensland woods that get all their food from the air and the moisture in the air. These orchids have no earth-roots, and use their claw-like roots to climb up trees.

2. Beginning, then, with those plants that do not need much help, we have to look at the **plants that scramble**. Most roses have a firm stem, but many of the climbing roses, like the white banksian rose, have prickles on their long exploring branches to help them to climb. The bramble also uses prickles to help it to clamber over a hedge; and as its stem is less firm than the banksian rose stem, it has many more prickles.

3. Still more help is needed by the **plants with twining stems**

like the hop, the honeysuckle, and the convolvulus. It is a pretty sight to watch a twiner that has got to the top of its pole and is throwing out its stems like feelers to seek for some new support. When it strikes some object it coils round it, and then drags up the stem. When a high wind comes and there is a heavy pull on the spiral, it acts as a spring. One calls out with wonder at the beautiful way in which these cables work. Some twining stems move from right to left, others from left to right. "But how," you ask, "can they move in a circle at all?"

4. **An experiment in twining**. Take a long dandelion flower-stem, break it off, and press one end to your tongue, and watch how it curls up. Or, still better, split a long stem and place it in a saucer of water. It coils up into pretty curls. If you remember what we learned about the sap-tubes you will understand this at once. We saw that the sap runs, not in the skin or outer bark, but just inside the bark. It is therefore the soft, inner part of the dandelion stem that sucks in the water freely, and, in trying to swell and lengthen, it curls round the outer skin which is not swollen in this way. Now, if we have a stem with one side growing faster than the other side, the same thing must happen; and this is probably what occurs in the case of the twining stem. One side grows faster than the other, and so the stem behaves in the same way as the dandelion stem, but more slowly. Often, as in the Victorian climbing lilac, several stems twine together and so are able, without other support, to raise their flowers much higher into the air than a single stem could. Some plants, again, like the clematis, use their leaf stalks for twining.

5. **Twining stems buried in wood**. Have you ever noticed a strong wire that has been twisted round a growing tree; how

it sinks deeper and deeper into the tree as the years pass and how it may even be buried in the wood? The same thing often happens to the woody stems of climbing plants. Think what happens. The root-sap is not checked in its upward flow by the wire, but when the leaf-sap flows down through the inner bark it is stopped when it reaches the wire. This check of the leaf-sap flow causes a strong growth of wood and bark just over the wire; for, as you remember, the leaf-sap is full of material for building and repairing. In this way, the upper lip may, in time, meet the lower lip of the wound, and then the wire is completely covered. After this, the tree grows freely again, and, in a few years, the wire is deep in the dead heartwood. But sometimes, the lips fail to join over the wire or the twining stem, and in this case the plant becomes feeble or even dies. Just as the folds of a great snake can choke an animal, so the rings of the climber may squeeze the life out of the plant.

6. Next, we come to **plants that climb by tendrils.** Look at a Virginia creeper, and you will see that a little branch has been changed into a kind of hand for climbing. If you look at a number of these tendrils, you may find one bearing a leaf, as if the tendril, in a moment of forgetfulness, had behaved like a branch. In the same way we know that the tendril of a grapevine is just a flower stalk changed into a hand, because we find grapes on the tendril. If the tendril of the Virginia creeper finds a piece of wire netting, it winds round it tightly; but if it touches a wall, the tendrils put out little discs that stick to the wall. Very pretty are the little green discs of the Japanese ivy creeper. These turn red after a time, and stick so firmly that they can hold up the weight of a very large plant. Try to pull them off, and you will

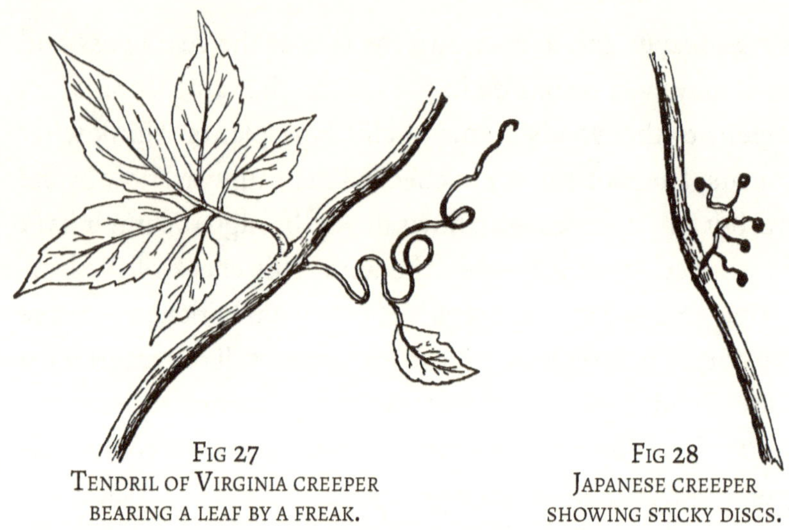

Fig 27
TENDRIL OF VIRGINIA CREEPER
BEARING A LEAF BY A FREAK.

Fig 28
JAPANESE CREEPER
SHOWING STICKY DISCS.

find that a thousand nails could not hold up the plant so well. With the help of these tiny discs, a single plant can cover the whole side of a large house.

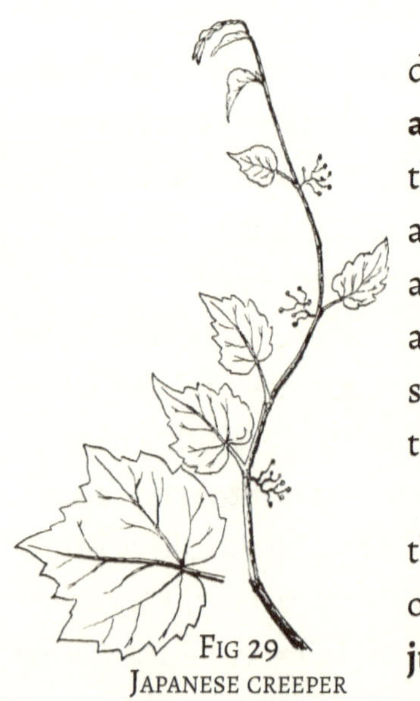

Fig 29
JAPANESE CREEPER
SHOWING AIR-ROOTS.

7. Similar to the plants with tendrils, are the **plants that climb by air-roots**, like the ivy. The ivy feeds through earth-roots and leaves, like another plant; but, by help of the air-roots, it is able to climb as high as a great tree without spending its strength in making a thick stem. Old trees are often smothered with ivy.

8. And now we come to plants that get food as well as support from other plants. **Plants that live on the juices of other plants.** Chief among such plants is one that gets up high

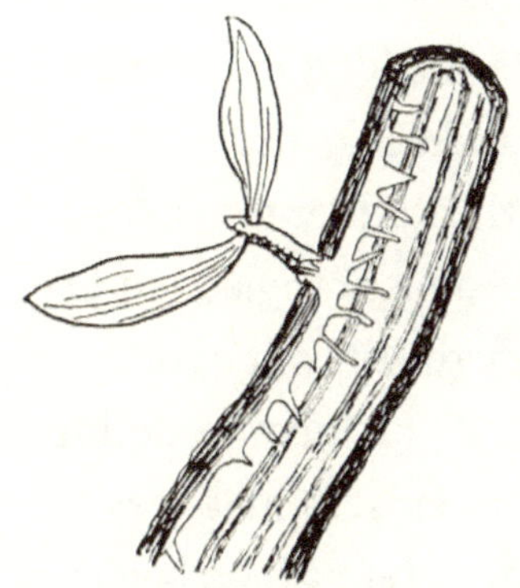

FIG 30
THE SUCKING ROOTS OF
A MISTLETOE SEEDLING.

in the air, not by climbing, but by help of the birds. You may see the mistletoe growing on gum trees, sheoaks, wattles, plum trees, oak trees, and even on pepper trees. The mistletoe bird eats the sweet seed of the mistletoe, and then perhaps passes to another branch or to another tree. It is a sticky seed, and on passing through the bird sticks to the branch on which he is seated. Then, if the seed can find a crack in the bark, it is able to germinate and strike its roots into the tree. In this way the mistletoe is able to suck food from the sap-tubes of the tree, while it also makes some food for itself by using its own leaves.

9. The mistletoe, you see, does a little work for itself; but the dodder is supported and fed entirely by the bush or grass round which it twines. It germinates indeed on the ground; but whenever it has twined round a bush, or a clover plant, the root dies, and it lives entirely by piercing and sucking the plant that

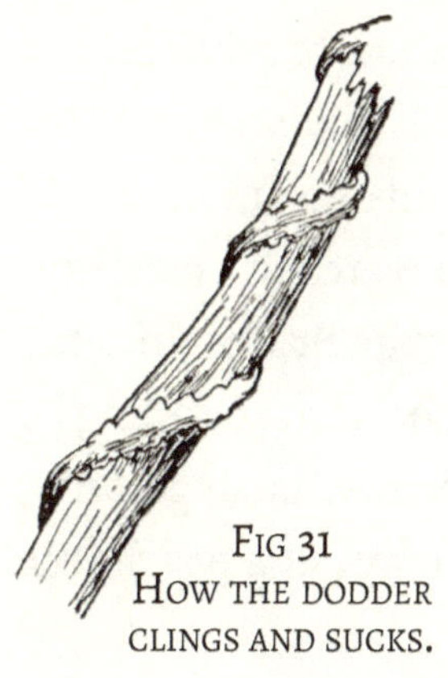

FIG 31
HOW THE DODDER
CLINGS AND SUCKS.

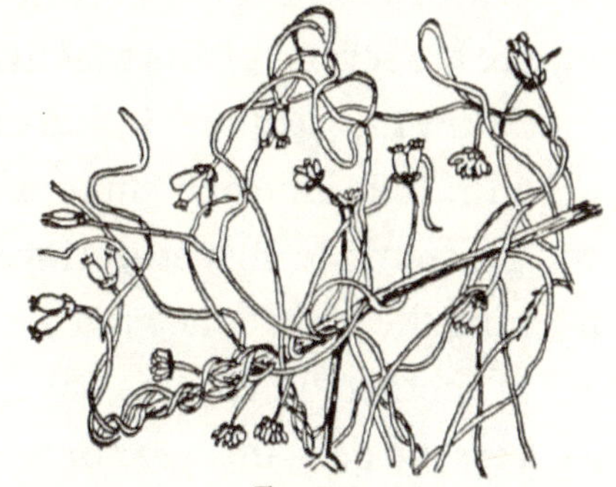

FIG 32
THE AUSTRALIAN SMOOTH SCRUB VINE, OR
DODDER LAUREL (AFTER VON MUELLER).

holds it up. It grows no leaves, and takes its food ready-made, just as the green fly does that pierces and sucks the rose-leaf. The dodder best known in Australia is the dodder that lives on lucerne. Many of you must have seen the dense tangled reddish masses of dodder that smother and suck the life out of lucerne plants. There are large tree-dodders; but the lucerne-dodder consists of slender, thread-like reddish stems. Sometimes the younger shoots of the dodder in groping for new food lay hold of and suck their own older shoots! Fig. 32 shows one of our scrub vines—the dodder laurel.

11. Another plant that makes no food for itself is the mushroom. Living on dead or dying roots and bulbs, the mushroom needs no green leaf in order to make food. Of still more interest to us is the rust in wheat and other plants. This is a minute plant that lives on the wheat, and does no work for itself. The rust on wheat alone is thought to cause a loss to Australia of £2,000,000 a year. There is a common orchid, too, that has no green leaves. This orchid, which bears a spike of flowers with red spots, lives largely on the roots of other plants. Just as the wire-worm and the grub of the cockchafer live on grass roots, so there are several plants that live on the roots of other plants.

12. **How the gardener imitates Nature**. The idea of budding or grafting one kind of plant on another kind of plant may have been got from the mistletoe. Have you ever watched a gardener fastening the bud of one kind of rose—say the Bride—into the bark of another kind of rose, say the Safranot? If the **budding** be a success, he gets, in a year or two, a **Bride** rose bush growing on **Safranot** roots[13]. In the same way, we may get a peach tree

13　　　　For budding and grafting see Chap. XXVI.

to grow on a plum tree root, if we think that the plum tree root is better fitted for a particular soil[14].

## Questions and Exercises:

(1)   Why do the prickles on the rose and the bramble point downwards?

(2)   How do the clematis and the nasturtium climb?

(3)   How do the following plants climb? Dolichos, any climbing rose, honeysuckle, grapevine, hop, passion-flower, sweet pea, native sarsaparilla.

(4)   Cut a shoot from a climber in full growth, and place it in a vessel of water. Note the direction in which the tip points, and, in an hour's time, note the different direction. Note how the passion-flower tendril turns at the lightest touch.

(5)   Letters of the alphabet cut in the wood of a tree are sometimes found buried deep in the trunk. Explain.

(6)   Try to find a climber whose stem is buried in whole or in part in the tree that supports it. Why is it that in the groove caused by a woody spiral climber the upper lip always bulges out more than the lower lip?

(7)   Look for an ivy shoot running along the ground and rooting. From what points in the stem do the roots spring? Compare the air-roots of the same plant.

(8)   One often sees a rose of one kind throwing up suckers of another kind from the root. Explain.

(9)   The cords attaching a tree to a stake should be examined occasionally. Why?

(10) One sometimes sees a gum tree branch dying back in the part above a mistletoe bush. Can you explain this?

(11)  Name any trees of your district on which the mistletoe may be found.

(12) An ivy plant may injure a tree in several ways. Can you name any?

---

14       Peaches and apricots are sometimes grown on plum tree roots when the soil is cold and wet.

(13) Note how a vine or pea tendril coils into a spiral and (after a few days) draws the plant nearer to its support.

(14) Watch the ways of a periwinkle plant, and tell what change you would need to make in it to turn it into a climbing plant.

**Composition Exercise.** — Tell the story of how an ivy-plant rose in the world without the help of a thick stem.

**Drawing Exercise.** — Draw (*a*) grapevine branch with tendril; (*b*) passion flower branch with tendril.

IX.

# The Leaves

<u>PART I.</u>

1. **How the leaf's air-food is made.** Many years ago, in the city of Calcutta, 146 English soldiers were thrust by their enemies into a small cellar. Fresh air could enter by one small window only, and the men fought to get near to this window. In the morning 123 were dead or dying—killed, not by gun nor by spear, but by breathing again and again their own breath!

2. Every man, woman, and child is making this poison-breath. They make it day and night without ceasing, from the moment they are born to the moment of death; and not only they, but every breathing animal on the face of the earth. Every fire, too, that is kindled, and every light that is lit, adds to this bad air. If nothing were done to remove this poison-breath, the whole air would soon be poisoned, and the world would become as deadly a place for us all as the Black Hole of Calcutta for those English soldiers.

3. **How the poison-breath is removed.** But the bad breath which is poison to man is just the food that the leaves need! Through a thousand tiny holes, too small to be seen, the poisoned air passes into the leaves. This bad air, which is death to us and life for the plants, is called carbon-dioxide, and is made up of

carbon and oxygen[15]. Now, I am going to prove to you that the air that we breathe out is this gas.

4. **What kind of gas does man breathe out?** First of all, you must know that when carbon-dioxide touches lime-water it makes it milky. Put some clear lime-water[16] into a clean tumbler. Breathe through a straw or reed into the water, and you will see it become milk-white. This proves that the air you breathe out is carbon-dioxide. And now I have to prove that every fire and light that is lit makes this poisonous gas.

5. **What kind of gas is made by lights?** Take a glass bottle with a narrow neck—a clean pickle bottle will do—and thrust into it the burning end of a taper. It will burn for a little, just as the soldiers in the cellar could live for a little; and then it will go out just as the soldiers' lives went out. The bottle has become for the taper what the Black Hole of Calcutta was for these men. To prove that the bottle is now full of the gas which you breathe out, pour into the bottle some clear lime-water, and shake it up. It becomes milky-white as before. In the same way, carbon-dioxide is made by every fire and light.

6. **Is there much carbon-dioxide in the air?** You will see, then, that a great deal of this gas must be made every day in houses and workshops and wherever there are men or animals or lights or fires; but the ocean of air that surrounds the globe is a vast one, and so the amount of carbon-dioxide near a plant is usually small. You can see this for yourself if you leave a glass

---

15        Strictly speaking, carbon-dioxide is not food, but food-material. The leaf is a factory for making plant-food, and the carbon-dioxide has to be mixed with fluids from the root before plant-food can be made.

16        To make lime-water, take a lump of lime twice the size of a hen's egg, and put it in a quart-bottle of water. Allow it to settle for a day or two, and then pour off the clear liquid into a clean glass bottle. Keep corked till it is needed.

jar of lime-water for a little in the air of the garden. A very thin, white scum forms on the top of the clear water. This is caused by the carbon-dioxide in the air. How little of this gas there is, is shown by the thinness of the scum.

7. **The chief aim of a plant.** You can see now why a tree requires to spread out many leaves in order to get as much of this air food as it needs. You can see, too, why there is such a struggle among the crowded grasses and among the trees in the thick "bush" to get up into the air. They are all seeking for a gas which is not plentiful. The great aim of a tree in putting out branches and leaves is to get as much food out of the air as possible.

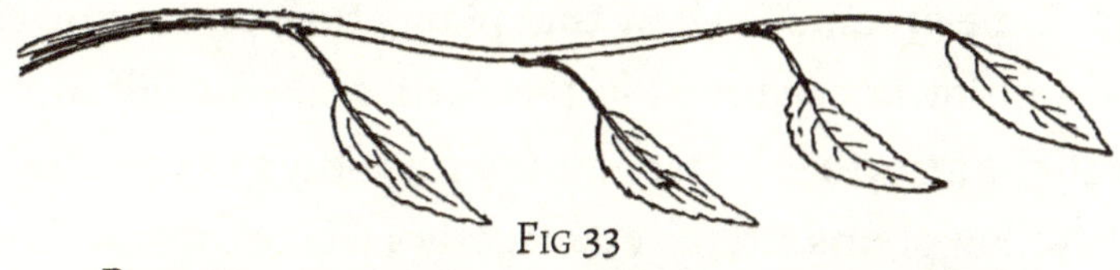

FIG 33

ROSE BRANCH IN SHADE OF NORTH FENCE; THE LEAVES ARE FAR APART AS IF TAKING LONG STEPS TO THE SUNLIGHT.

8. **The leaves without light cannot make air-food.** Just as a ship carries as much sail as it can, so a tree carries as many leaves as it can. If you could spread out all the leaves of a great tree on the ground, side by side, you would be astonished at the great amount of space covered. But there is something needed by the leaves that the sails do not need. This is sunlight.

FIG 34

BRANCH (FROM SAME ROSEBUSH AS IN FIG 33) THAT HAS OVERTOPPED THE FENCE AND GOT INTO THE SUNLIGHT.

9. **Catching sunlight.** Without the help of the sun the leaf can get no food out of the air. Below the thin skin on the upper side of the leaf there is a soft, living green-stuff which, with the sun's help, makes food for the plant. The carbon in the poison-gas is kept for the plant's use, and the oxygen is allowed to go into the air again.

You will see, then, that the leaves take out of the air a gas which is poisonous to us, and that they return to the air a gas which is good for us[17]. We can understand better now why our seedlings bent towards the sun when we put them near a window.

10. **Experiments to shew that plants turn to the sun.** Grow some sunflower seedlings in the dark, and you will find that though the growth is faster, it is not a healthy growth. The long, weak, yellow stems stretch out eagerly as if seeking for the sun. The seed-leaves, too, can hardly open, and, when they do open, are small. It is clear, then, that leaves are made for the sun, and can do no good without it.

11. Watch a healthy, young sunflower plant that has reached its third pair of leaves. Observe these leaves after dark, and see how they droop when their lord the sun is gone. If you cover the plant with a box that admits no light, they will behave in the same way. And now, watch a young sunflower that is forming

---

17       It is important to note that this is only part of the truth. Plants, like all other living things, breathe, that is consume oxygen, and give off carbon dioxide. This process during daylight is slight as compared with the contrary process; but during the night the breathing of plants vitiates the air in the same way as the breathing of animals. After the process of leaf-feeding has been made clear, the process of leaf-breathing should be explained. A plant feeds that it may work. In feeding it gives out oxygen; in working it destroys oxygen. To test this, place a handful of peas that have been soaking for 24 hours in a bottle. Cork tightly. The germinating peas will give off carbon dioxide. Prove by thrusting the lighted end of a taper into the bottle. All this shows that plants should not be kept in bedrooms.

a flower-head. See how all the leaves near the flower-head are drawn into a kind of rosette, and how they all follow the sun round. Even the stem that bears them moves round. Still later, when the plant has many flowers, note how the flowers look to the sun in the morning and see the last of him in the evening, and how, after dark, the flowers droop and look towards the earth.

12. Most plants, when they have passed the growing period, fix their leaves in the position where they are likely to get most light. On cloudy days, a leaf with its face turned full to the sky receives most light. This will help you to understand the leaves of many English trees.

<u>Questions and Exercises.</u>

(1) Explain why you soon become stupid and sleepy in a room which is not well-aired.

(2) Why is air purer in a garden or wood than in a street?

(3) Explain why a lamp goes out or burns badly if you fill up the holes at the base of the lamp.

(4) The leaves of the ordinary mallow weed are sensitive to the light and follow the sun round. Put a stick into the ground in a line with the midrib of one of the leaves on the morning of a sunny day. Place another stick in a line with the same midrib in the evening. Note the angle that the leaf has passed through.

*Note.* — The leaf must be one that swings clear of the ground and of the other leaves. Leaves that are in the way can be removed.

(5) Compare the day-position and the night-position of the leaves of the nasturtium and the lupine.

(6) Some flowers shut early in the day, others later. Linnaeus, a great botanist, tried to make a dial of flowers that would tell in this way the time of day. Name some flowers that shut when rain is threatening; or in the evening.

(7) Fig. 33 shows a rose-shoot growing in the deep shade of a fence.

Fig. 34 shews a shoot of the same rose that has overtopped the fence. Explain why the one runs to stem and the other to leaf.

(8) "Laying" of wheat is due to the plants being so crowded that the stems get too little light. This makes the stems weak. Try to see cases of this kind.

**Composition Exercise.** — But for the plants, the air would soon be poisonous to us. Explain this.

**Drawing Exercise.** — Draw (*a*) a seedling grown in the light; (*b*) a seedling of the same kind, grown in the dark. Or draw (*a*) sunflower by day; (*b*) sunflower after sunset, or after being put in a dark place.

## X.

# The Leaves

<u>PART II.</u>

1. **A plant is mostly built up from air and water.** We have seen that the work of getting food out of the air is done by the living green stuff in the leaf with the help of the sun. The leaf must also have the help of water: you know how a leaf wilts if it does not get enough water. This water comes from the root which sends up also the lime and nitrogen and other foods that the leaves cannot get out of the air.

2. But the greater part of the plant-food is got from the air by the leaves. You can see this for yourself every time you burn a dried plant. The bush disappears into the air, leaving only a little ash. The bush was built up mostly out of the air, and therefore most of it passes again into the air. The nitrogen and any water still left in the bush escape also into the air; and the little heap of ash that remains shews us how small is the amount of other food that the plant got from the earth[18]. Indeed, as we have seen, there are plants, like the forest orchids of Queensland,

---

18        Behind Professor Nobbe's Forest School in Saxony there are trees that have been grown in huge glass jars of water. Into this water once a month are placed measured amounts of nitrogen and the other root-food. Though the roots have never been in touch with earth, the trees have thriven for over a quarter of a century. Experiments of a similar kind are said to have shown that out of every 100 lb. of wheat harvested, only 1 lb. is from the soil. The rest is from air and water.

that do not touch the earth at all, but get all their food from air and moisture. Look also at the elk-horn fern which you see so often growing on the walls of houses.

3. The solid food got by the root, though not great in amount, is important; and the plant cannot live without it. All plants need the same air-food, but they differ greatly in the kind of root-food they need. Soils, too, differ greatly in the kind of root-food they can give, and this is why we find some kinds of weeds or trees plentiful in clay land, and other kinds in light soil: one kind in rich, deep soil, and another kind in poor soil. Fix firmly in your mind, however, the fact that the plant is built up mostly from food got from air and water.

4. **The wonder of it all.** Think of the largest gum tree you know. How wonderful that it should be built up out of something that you cannot see: the invisible made visible! What wonder-workers the little leaves are that glance in the sun and flutter in the breeze! How hard they must work to build up those mighty towers of branch and leaf.

5. **How the plant turns dead stuffs into living foods.** And did you ever think how strange it is that the leaf is able to feed on dead things that you could not live on. All the food you eat was once alive, but the plants can eat carbon and lime and other things that were never alive. The plants turn these dead things into living food that the animals can eat. The wheat plant turns these dead things into bread, which is the staff of life for man. Follow the steps clearly in your mind—from the dead stuffs up to the body of man. Sometimes we make use of the lower animals to help us to get the living food we need. The grass eats the dead earth-foods and air-foods; the cow turns the grass

into milk; and we turn the cow's milk into human bodies. You see, then, how much depends on the leaf. Our lives depend on it; the lives of our horses and cows and dogs depend on it. The leaf is as useful as it is beautiful.

6. **The leaf cannot travel to seek food.** Now, this wonderful worker—the leaf—is not able to travel in search of food; it must stay in one place. It cannot fly like a swallow, seeking its food in the air. It has to wait for the food that happens to come floating by on the air-currents, just as the sea-flower—the anemone— has to wait till the current of water brings some little shrimp or shell-fish within its reach. When you remember how little carbon there is in the air[19], you will see that a great tree has need of many leaves to catch food for it; for you must never forget that every living part of the tree, from the topmost twig to the lowest root, lives on the food that the leaf makes.

7. We must now look **inside** the leaf, and see how it is able to do this wonderful work. And here you must allow me to look through the microscope and tell you what I see.

8. **The inside of a leaf.** The upper skin of the leaf (fig. 35) is made up of little cells full of water. This part of the leaf is without colour. The green colour shines through the skin from the long cells which you see below the skin. These two rows of long cells are full of living green stuff. Look well at the inside of a leaf. Below the upper skin a, are cells of living green stuff b. Beneath these is the spongy part c, where the surplus water evaporates. In the lower skin d are many breathing pores. These are shown in Fig. 36. It is here that the starch, sugar, and other stuffs are made that the plant is built of. All the carbon collected by the leaf's

19    In 2000 cubic feet of air there is only one cubic foot of carbon dioxide.

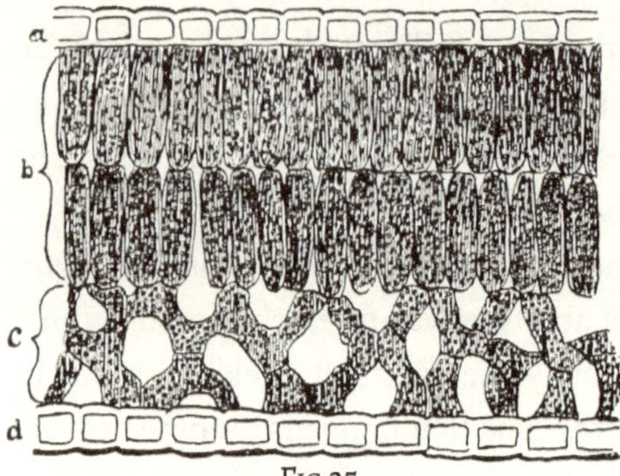

FIG 35

THE INSIDE OF A LEAF. BELOW THE UPPER SKIN
A, ARE CELLS FULL OF GREEN STUFF B. BENEATH
THESE IS THE SPONGY PART C, WHERE THE
BREATHING GOES ON. IN THE LOWER SKIN D ARE
MANY BREATHING PORES. THESE ARE SHOWN
MUCH LARGER THAN THEY REALLY ARE.

skin, and all the matter gathered by the root, are passed on to these green cells; just as all the food we eat is passed on to the stomach. And, indeed, this part of the leaf is the plant's stomach.

9. **How water escapes from the leaf.** Below the closely-packed green cells you see looser cells which fill up the space between the green cells and the under-skin. This is the place where water leaves the leaf, after having done its work. When you water a piece of land, you have to see that the water can get away from the land after passing through it. If you do not attend to this, the land may soon be a useless bog. Well, this spongy part of the leaf is the place where the water from the root leaves the plant. You see in Fig. 36 little doors in the lower skin where the water goes out in the form of vapour. These openings look like mouths, but we shall call them breathing-pores[20].

10. **The breathing-pores.** Every leaf has many of these openings, and some have many thousands of them. On every square inch of either side of a blue gum leaf there are 22,000 of them. When the plant has plenty of water, the breathing-pores are kept wide open, and evaporation goes on quickly; but in dry

20        Stomatas.

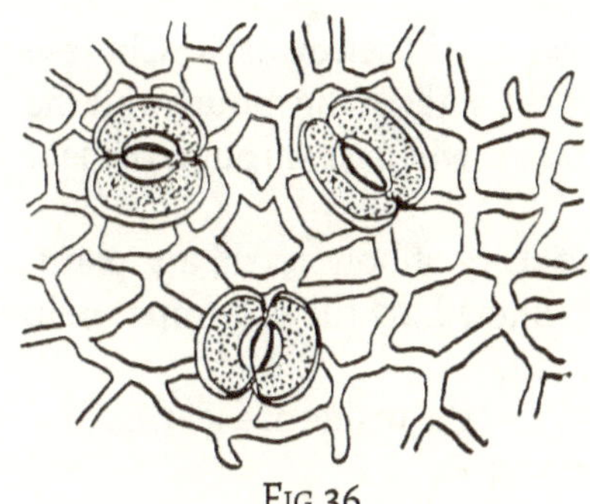

FIG 36
THE LOWER SKIN OF A LEAF
SHOWING THE BREATHING PORES.

weather, when the plant needs all its moisture, the openings are closed. In order to prevent evaporation going on too quickly, the breathing-pores are in the lower skin. This is nearly always the case where the leaf holds its upper face to the sun; but in leaves, like the gum tree leaf, that hang downwards, both sides have breathing-pores.

## Questions and Exercises.

(1) Shew how in a tree we have the invisible made visible.

(2) Wood ashes make excellent manure. Why is this?

(3) Why is it important to keep the leaves of a plant free from dust?

(4) Early in summer a cherry tree is stripped of its leaves by the **pear slug**. This hurts the tree in several ways. Mention any.

(5) How does the elk-horn fern live? Why does it grow best in a moist air?

**Stomata.**

(6) Breathing-pores are usually found on the under side of leaves; but in water plants that rest on the surface of the water they are found only on the upper side. Why?

(7) Why are there breathing-pores on both sides of a gum tree leaf?

(8) Breathing-pores are not generally found on stems and spines. The gorse is an exception. Why?

(9) Where would you expect to find the breathing-pores in a prickly pear plant? In a cactus?

(10) Cactuses and other desert plants have few breathing-pores. Why is this?

(11) A lilac leaf has 160,000 breathing-pores for every square inch. A mistletoe leaf has only 200 per square inch. Why has the mistletoe so few?

(12) Experiment to shew that air escapes through the breathing-

pores of a leaf. Get a leaf of the primrose, or still better, of the Chinese primrose, with a clean-cut stalk. Place the stalk in the mouth and the blade in water. Blow into the stalk, and air will pass through the leaf into the water.

**Composition Exercise.** — Tell the story of how earth, air, plant, and sun all work to make you bread. Shew how the cow must help before you can get butter with the bread.

**Drawing Exercise.** — Draw from Fig. 35 the inside of a leaf. Colour the cells that contain the living green stuff.

XI.

# The Leaves

<u>PART III.</u>
SOME EXPERIMENTS.

1. We saw that the living green stuff in the leaf makes starch, sugar, and other materials that the plant needs. That the plant makes sugar you know well; for you taste it every time you eat a cherry or a bunch of grapes, or bite the honey-tube of the nasturtium. Starch also you know well; for the Indian corn-flour used for puddings is almost pure starch. Potatoes, too, are made almost entirely of starch. Some of the starch is stored up in thick roots, some in bulbs, some in underground stems, some in twigs, and some also—as we saw in the case of wheat, in the seed. When the leaf has made more starch than it can hold, it passes it down to the stem. If you tear a leaf off, and put the stalk in water, it will go on making starch, but soon has to stop because it can no longer pass the starch down to the stem. During the night, when a leaf cannot work for want of light, the starch flows down into twig and stem, and so the leaf is almost free of starch when the morning light calls it to another day's work.

2. **An experiment to show that there is starch in a potato.** Now, there is an easy way of finding out whether there is starch

75

in any substance. When moist starch is touched by iodine[21], it becomes black with a blue tinge. You can prove that there is starch in a potato by scraping some of the cut surface into pulp, and then applying a little tincture of iodine. In a similar way, starch can be found in any quickly growing leaf that has been at work in the sun. This experiment is too difficult for you just now, but you can easily prove that leaves that are not green can make no starch.

3. **Experiment to shew that a white leaf can make no starch.** Take a white leaf—you can often find one on a geranium that is in a shady spot—and cut into the surface gently so as to make a network of cuts. Steep the leaf in a tincture of iodine. Then rinse in water and you will see that there is no sign of starch. This shews that a leaf that has no living green stuff cannot make starch. Plants like the mushroom that have none of this green stuff live on the food stored up by green-leaved plants.

4. Nor can a leaf that gets no sunlight make starch. This can be proved by testing the leaves of a plant that has been kept in the dark for a few days, but this also is too difficult for you just now.

5. You have heard that all the forces that we use—steam force, water force, and so on—are got from the sun. So also, you can now see, is the force that is stored up by the plant in starch. When you eat the starch in a potato, you are taking in the sun-force that enables you to run about. When a plant pushes out shoots, it does it by sun-force; and the horse that eats the plant obtains the force—sun-force, that enables it to gallop round the field. Every grain of starch won by the leaf is

21      Tincture of iodine can be got at a trifling cost from a chemist, or crystals of iodine can be dissolved in alcohol. Iodine is poisonous.

so much sun-force ready to be packed away in twig or stem or root or seed for present work or future work[22]. On a sunny day, a strong vegetable-marrow plant takes in sun-force so quickly that you can almost see the plant growing.

6. Try to see in your mind what is going on in that marrow plant. Ten thousand root-cells are receiving water and passing it up and on; through a million breathing pores the water is escaping into the air; through a million mouths the leaves are taking in air-food; at a thousand points the work goes on of building new roots, new cells, new buds, new shoots, new flowers, new marrow-fruits... What a scene of busy work! And all done by sun-force! The marrow is a beautiful living sun-machine.

7. In making starch, the leaf does two good things for us; it uses up the carbon that was poisoning the air, and it sets free the oxygen which is life-giving to man. No one has eyes sharp enough to see the oxygen that is passing continually into the air from every leaf that is at work in the sunlight, but you can easily see the oxygen that passes off from a water-plant.

8. **Experiment to shew that leaves give off oxygen.** Take a leafy water-plant in full growth and place it in a glass bottle. The glass must be clear and the water clean. Place the bottle where it will get the sunlight, and notice how the bubbles of gas collect on the leaves and how they grow in size till they break away and rise to the surface. If you place one of the plants upside down with the cut stem below the surface of the water, you may see the bubbles of gas coming freely from the cut end[23]. This gas has

---

22    A beautiful demonstration of sun-force can be given by the radiometer. This is a very small machine like a windmill, but driven, not by the wind, but by the impact of the sun's rays.

23    If the water be boiled, the carbonic acid gas in the water is driven off. There is then

been tested, and found to be oxygen. When the plant is removed into a duller light, the bubbles do not rise so fast. What does this mean? On a cloudy day, too, less gas is thrown off than on a bright day. When the plant is put in a place where there is no light at all, no bubbles are made. What does this prove?

10. **Experiment to shew that leaves give off water**. Take a number of freshly cut leaves; place them on a level surface, and cover them with a glass jar or a bell-glass. In a short time you will see the water vapour beginning to make the inner surface of the glass dim; and after a few hours water drops will form. Since you cannot see the water passing off from the leaves, it is clear that the water is given off by the leaf in the form of water vapour. But you may say that these leaves were cut, and that the water may have come from the cut stalks. Well, let us try the same experiment with an uncut plant. Take a small pot-plant and cover the pot and the earth tightly with some oil-cloth or oiled paper or sheet rubber. Tie this covering so that no moisture can escape from the pot or the earth. Then cover the plant with a bell-jar. The glass will become dim, and the water drops will form as before.

*Note.* — Experiment to prove the presence of starch in any strongly growing leaves: If the leaves be placed for a few minutes in boiling water, and then for a short time in warm alcohol, the green colouring matter will disappear. Then place the leaves for a few hours in a dilute alcoholic solution of iodine. Then rinse in water, and place in a saucer full of water. The dark or dark bluish colour will shew the presence of starch.

no food for the leaves, and the bubbles of oxygen cease to form.

## Questions and Exercises.

(1) If you leave a board on grass for a few days, what effect has it on the colour? Explain.

(2) The variegated Danubian reed—bamboo (i.e., the variety with white bands running up the leaves) does not grow so vigorously as the ordinary green variety. How is this?

(3) Leaves cut for fodder in the evening are richer in starch than leaves cut in the morning. How?

(4) When you store up force in a clock by winding it up, you know that you will get back the same amount of force in the clock's movement. How does a grain of starch resemble a clock that has been wound up?

(5) Tell any of the kinds of work by which a plant uses the sun-force that it has stored up.

**Composition Exercise**. — Tell how the plant stores up sun-force, and how by sun-force a pony can run, and by sun-force you can ride on its back.

*Note*. — A distinction should be made between the bodily force and the spirit force of a man. We cannot trace a man's spirit force to the sun; nor, indeed, can we explain any form of life force by physical causes alone.

**Drawing Exercise**. — Draw the fruit of a vegetable marrow when it is just forming, and, alongside of it, a full-grown marrow-fruit. Mark the dates, so as to shew how quickly the marrow grows.

XII.

# The Leaves

<u>PART IV.</u>

SHAPES AND VEIN-PLANS.

1. Now that we know what leaves have to do for the plant, we can go on to look at the form that leaves take. And the first part to look at is the stalk of the leaf.

2. **The leaf-stalk.** The leaf-stalk may be long when it is necessary to hold the blade well out into light; or it may be short when this is not needed. Again, the leaf-stalk is strong when the blade is heavy, or slight when the leaf is light. Where the blade is heavy, the stalk may have a broad, firm hold upon the stem, or may even clasp the stem. Look how a rhubarb stalk clasps the stem, and you will see how a great blade is supported. Examine a number of leaf-stalks and you will find that they are rarely round. Often, as in the violet, they have two ridges that form a channel or groove. Why is this? If you look at the girders that are used for supporting buildings, you will see that we have copied this plan of Nature. We have found that a round iron rod placed across a stream will not bear the weight of a bridge so well as a girder. By using this plan for umbrella-ribs, we lessen the weight and increase the strength. You will find a good example of the plan in the palm-tree leaf, which is one of

the heaviest of leaves. How strongly a leaf holds on to the stem you will find out if you try to pull one off.

3. **The leaf-blade.** A leaf that turns its face to the sun to catch the light is generally flat and broad. In a leaf-blade like this, the upper side differs in look from the underside. We have seen that the upper and under sides have different kinds of work to do; and from our peep inside of a leaf, perhaps you can guess why the lower surface is of a lighter green than the upper surface.

4. A leaf, on the other hand, that holds itself erect in the air is generally long and narrow, and has the same look on both sides. Such a leaf looks alike on both sides because both do the same kind of work. Large, broad leaves would be out of place in a meadow where a thousand plants are trying to get up into the light; and so we find that grasses have generally long, narrow erect leaves. Notice, too, that some of these small plants that are much crowded have leaves cut into a fine network of leaflets. For shrubs and trees that have to stand up in the wind, these deeply-cut leaves would not be strong enough; and so in high shrubs and in trees we generally have leaves that are not deeply cut[24]. The leaf, you see, must have strength enough to keep its place in the air. This thought leads us to examine the blade to see how the leaf is made strong.

5. **The leaf's skeleton**. Tear off from the stem the leaf of a sow-thistle, and you will see that the stalk gets its strength from several woody sap-tubes that pass along it. These tough tubes run on into the blade of the leaf, and are split up into a network of veins that form the skeleton. Examine a skeleton

24      This applies particularly to the soft-leaved deciduous plants that cast their leaves every year. Among the plants that hold their leaves through the winter there are many exceptions, as the wattles. Evergreens have tough leaves that can stand the wind.

leaf—a leaf in which the soft parts have rotted away, leaving only the hard parts. On this framework or skeleton, the soft parts of the leaf are spread.

6. **How the root-sap spreads over the leaf.** Have you ever seen a field that was being watered from a main channel? The water leaves the main stream for smaller channels, and from these runs into still smaller channels, until the whole land is soaked. In a similar way, the root-sap flows from the large veins to the small veins, and is thus spread all over the leaf. We saw how the root sap-tubes run up through the new wood into the leaf. This root-sap enters the leaf along the upper part of the veins. Can you guess from your peep inside of a leaf why the root-sap spreads over the upper part of the leaf? When the smallest veins have been reached, the sap begins to flow back through the under part of the veins. You will notice that the veins stand out from the under surface of the leaf, while they are sunk slightly into the upper surface. If the edge of the leaf be torn, this beautiful plan for the coming and going of the sap is spoiled. Can this be the reason why the leaf of a gum tree has a vein that runs all round the leaf a little in from

Fig 133

Edge-vein of gum tree leaf.

the edge (fig. 123)? Even when the edge is broken, the vein-plan is not disturbed. Now, owing to the long life of a gum tree leaf, it is often broken at the edge or bitten by insects. Look at a number of fallen gum tree leaves, and you will see that the insect often stops at the edge-vein. If you have ever reared moths, you will have noticed that small caterpillars often avoid veins in the leaves they eat.

7. **How the leaf-sap returns to the stem.** You have often watched, on the playground, how little streams of rain gather into larger streams, and these into still larger till the gutter is reached. In a similar way, the sap that has flowed over the leaf flows back into the veins and the ribs and the stalk and, at last, into the stem. The root-sap has now been mixed with the air-food caught by the leaf, and is therefore no longer root-sap. It is now leaf-sap; and it is ready to build up wood and bark, bud and root. It no longer flows in the new wood, but down the inner bark.

8. **The shapes of leaves.** And now we are ready to think about the different vein plans in different kinds of leaves. Walk through a large garden, and look at nothing else but the shapes of the leaves and the plans of the veins. How are they shaped? In a thousand ways, you say. True; but if you look again, you will see that most of them are feather-like in the way the veins run. Look at the feather in fig. 37 and compare it with the leaf shewn on fig. 38. The plan in both is a number of side-ribs running from a strong mid-rib.

9. Take now an oak leaf (fig. 39). Here we have, as before, the side-veins running from a mid-rib, but the leaf looks as if you had cut bits out from the margin. If it had been

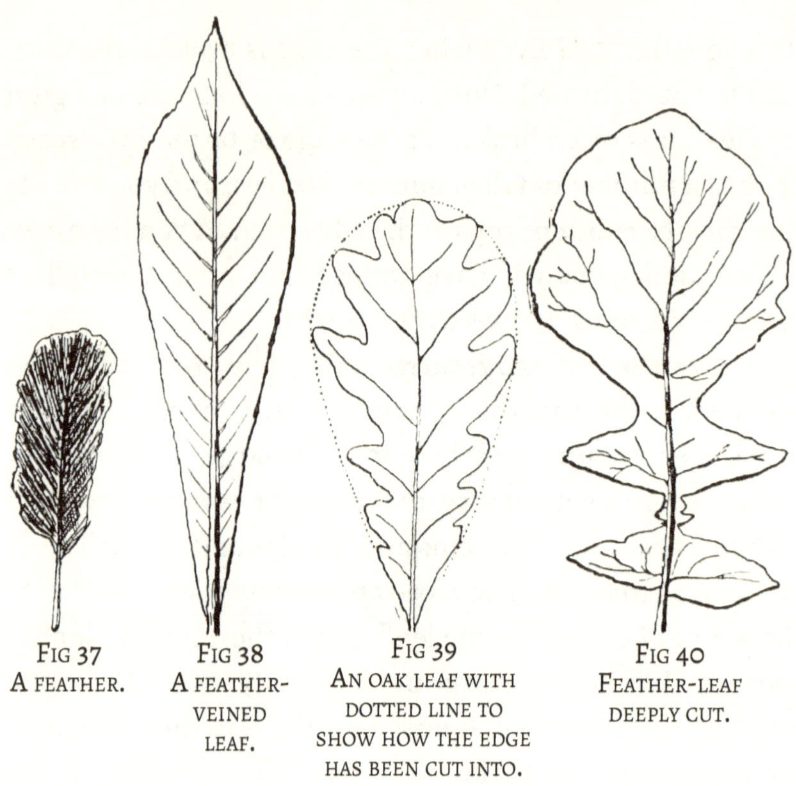



uncut like the leaf in fig. 38, it would have had the shape which I have traced by dotted lines. In some plants the leaf is more deeply cut (fig. 40); but in this case, too, the plan of the skeleton is the same: a mid-rib that sends off side-ribs. Sometimes the cuts in the leaf are so deep that they reach the mid-rib, and then we have leaves like the pepper tree leaf (fig. 41). This looks very different from the leaf we started with; but the plan of the veins is still the same—a number of side-ribs running from a strong mid-rib. The pepper tree leaf, therefore, like the oak leaf, is feather-like. We have now, you see, got a name that will cover a great number of leaves

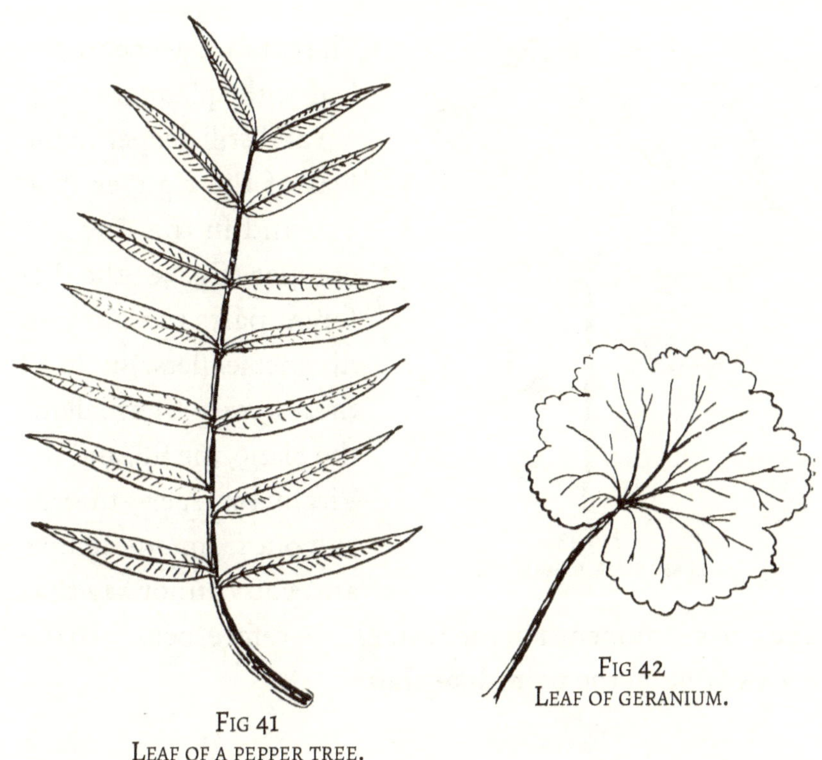



which, at first sight, look quite different. We shall call all these the **feather-like leaves**.

10. But now you bring to me a geranium leaf and say that you cannot "find the feather" in it. All the ribs run from the same point in the leaf-stalk, just as all the fingers of the hand rise from the palm. Also, the mid-rib is not stronger than the other ribs. Well, we shall call this kind of skeleton the palm-like plan.

11. Already I hear you asking: Are the leaves on the palm-like plan cut into in the same way as those that are on the feather-plan? Yes, they are cut in many ways. If you look for a mallow weed (fig. 43), you will see how the cutting begins.

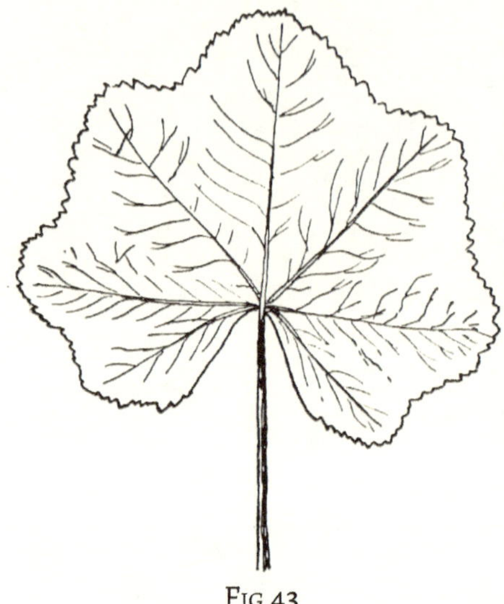

FIG 43
LEAF OF MALLOW-WEED.

The cuts are deeper in the leaf of the plane tree (fig. 44) and still deeper in the leaf of the fig tree (fig. 45), and in the Virginia creeper (fig. 46) the different parts run out into distinct leaflets. But in all these leaves—the mallow, the plane, the fig, and the Virginia creeper—the ribs run out from one centre, and you cannot say that one rib is stronger than the rest. All, therefore, belong to the leaves built on the **palm-like plan**[25].

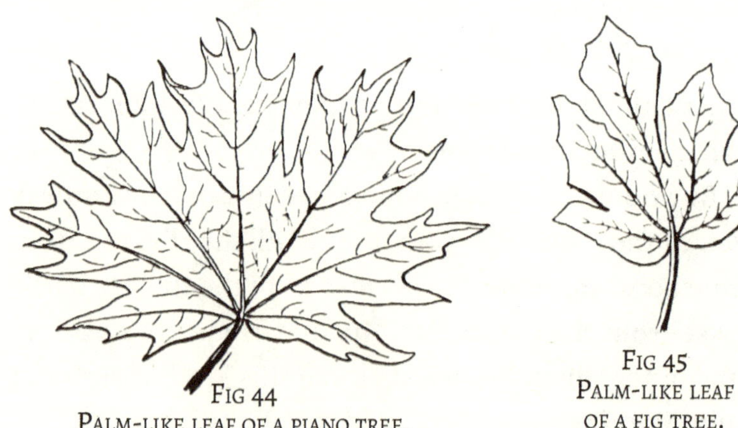

FIG 44
PALM-LIKE LEAF OF A PIANO TREE.

FIG 45
PALM-LIKE LEAF
OF A FIG TREE.

**12. Leaves named according to how the edge is cut.** Leaves are named not only according to the way in which the ribs run,

25     In some leaves the feather- and palm-plans are combined.

but according to the way in which the leaf is cut. If the leaf is not cut at all, as in an upper leaf of the ivy, it is called **entire** (fig. 47); if it is cut like the edge of a saw, it is called **saw-edged**; if the cuts are deeper, as in the oak, it is called **toothed**; if still more cut into, as in fig. 45, it is called **lobed**; if very deeply cut, as in cosmos, it is said to be dissected. Often, the leaf is so edged that one word cannot describe it.

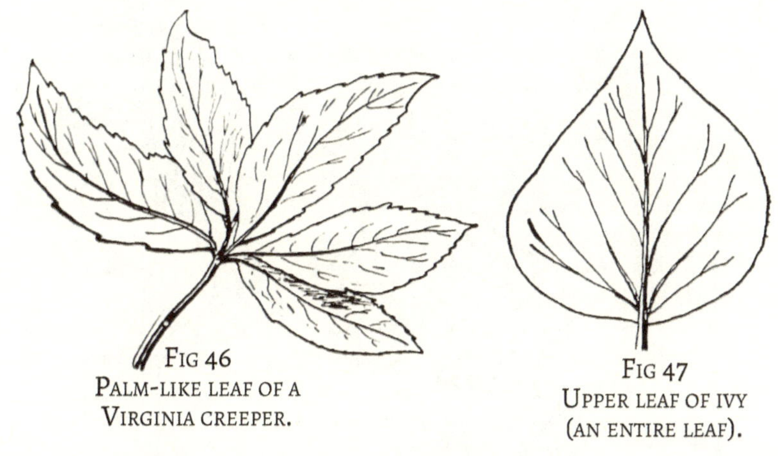

Fig 46
Palm-like leaf of a
Virginia creeper.

Fig 47
Upper leaf of ivy
(an entire leaf).

13. **Leaves named according to their shape—as a whole**. When you look at a leaf as a whole, you can often compare it in shape to a heart, or to an egg, to a **spear-head** or an **arrow-head**, or some other well-known thing. Some are so narrow as to be called **hair-like**, others so round as to be like a round **shield**. People do not always agree as to what a leaf is like in shape: and if you look carefully, and call it by some object you know, you need not trouble though your name is not the one given in some book.

14. **Leaves named according to their position on the stem.**

Some leaves, again, as those of the periwinkle, are set on the stem in pairs opposite to one another, and these are called **opposite leaves** (fig. 51). In a few plants, several leaves spring out at one

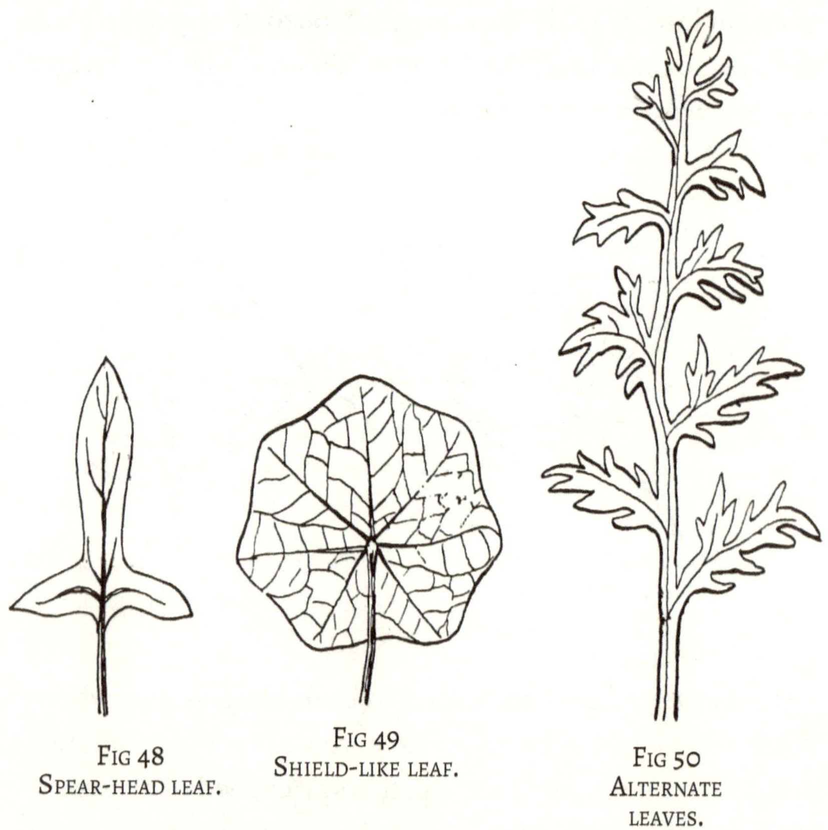

FIG 48
SPEAR-HEAD LEAF.

FIG 49
SHIELD-LIKE LEAF.

FIG 50
ALTERNATE
LEAVES.

point, all round the stem, making a kind of leaf-wheel which is called a **whorl** (fig. 52).

15. Some leaves again are **smooth**, others **hairy**. The hairs differ much on different leaves, so that some feel **rough** as you touch them, others **soft**, and others **velvety**.

16. When a leaf is cut up into distinct leaflets, it is called a

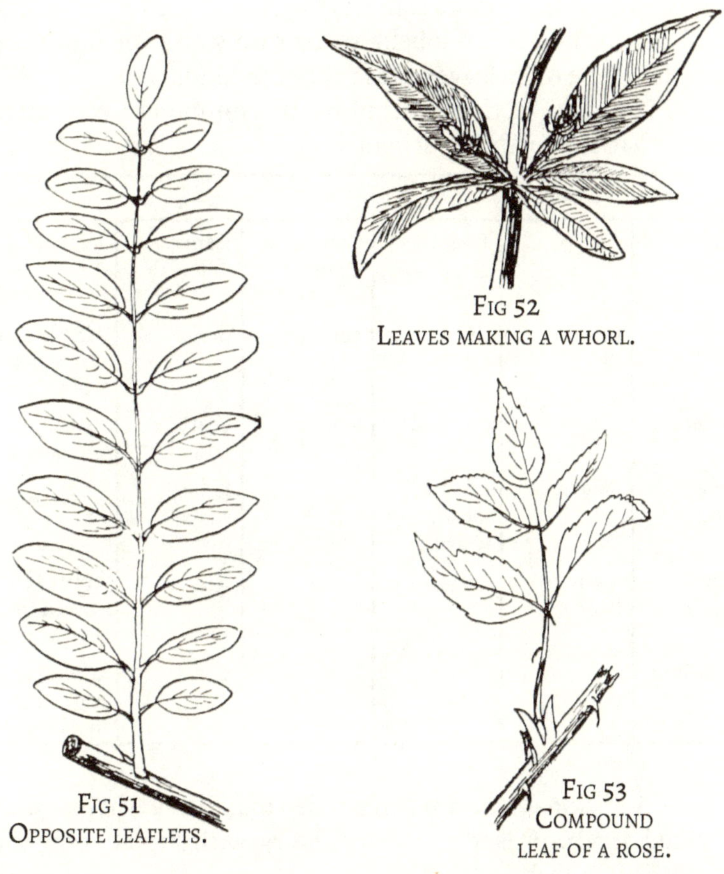

FIG 52
LEAVES MAKING A WHORL.

FIG 51
OPPOSITE LEAFLETS.

FIG 53
COMPOUND
LEAF OF A ROSE.

**compound leaf** (fig. 53); if less cut than this, as in the fig tree (fig. 45), it is called a **simple leaf**.

## Questions and Exercises.

(1) To what rib-plan do the following leaves belong? Plane, jasmine, violet, gum tree, silver wattle, golden wattle, geranium, periwinkle, tomato, hollyhock, snapdragon, grape vine, clover, rose, castor oil plant, lippin?

(2) Explain how and why the leaf of the plane tree is so strongly attached to the stem.

(3) The dock has a large leaf; how is the leaf stalk strengthened?

(4) When the garden lobelia throws up stalks for flowering, it alters the shape of its leaves. Describe both kinds.

(5) Make a list of the leaves of plants common in your district, according to the following scheme:

| LEAVES | | | | | |
|---|---|---|---|---|---|
| Name. | Ribs plan. | Edges plan. | Simple or Compound. | General Shape. | Remarks. |
| Rose | feather-like | saw-edged | compound | oval | 3 leaflets; in strong leaves 5 or 7 |
| Violet | " | notched | simple | heart | 1 stalk; grooved |
| Geranium | palm-like | notched, lobed, wavy | " | kidney-shaped | " |
| Honeysuckle | feather-like | entire | " | oval | upper side curved inwards |
| Red Gum | " | " | " | sickle | a vein runs round the edge |

*Note.* Additional columns can be used to indicate whether the leaf is stalked or non-stalked, smooth or hairy, with stipules or without, alternate or opposite.

XIII.

# The Leaves

<u>PART V.</u>

REASONS FOR LEAF-SHAPES.

1. We have looked at the feather-like leaf and at the palm-like leaf; and now we have to look at another kind.

2. **The grass-leaf type.** If you look at a grass-leaf, you will find that the ribs do not run either on the feather-plan or the palm-plan, but run from the bottom to the top of the leaf either in a straight line or in a curved line (fig. 54). Even the small veins run in this way, so that there is no network of veins. This is the plan for all the grasses. You can see this clearly if you hold up to the light a leaf of the Danubian reed, a blade of buffalo grass, or of prairie-grass. Notice that though there are no side-ribs, there is sometimes a distinct mid-rib to make the blade firm.

3. This is the plan also for all the lilies, and, indeed, for all plants that have only one seed-leaf. Look at a narcissus, a gladiolus, the harbinger of spring, or any other of the bulb-rooting plants among the wild flowers. Leaves on this plan rarely have any leaf-stalk, and they are seldom deeply cut into.

4. And now if you ask me why the leaf of one plant is on one plan, and the leaf of a second plant on a different plan, I cannot always tell you; but the reason can be guessed in some cases.

91

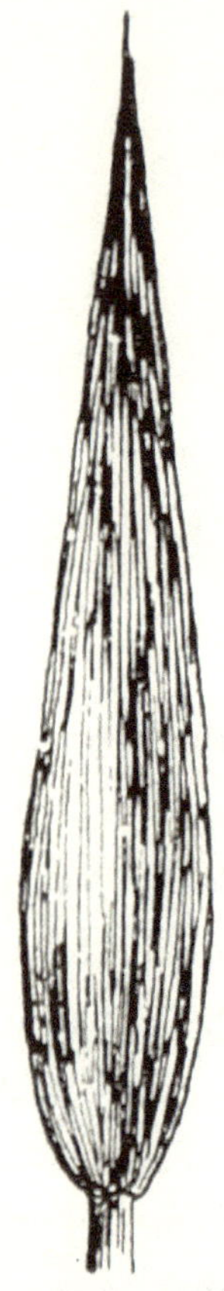

Fig 54.
Leaf of a plant
with one
seed-leaf.

5. **How light shapes the leaves.** Leaves of pond-plants are generally finely cut or long and ribbon-like if they live under the surface; but if they live on the surface of the water, like the water-lily, they become broad and are uncut. This may be due to the fact that water shuts off a good deal of light. Experiments show that leaves become narrower as the light upon them is lessened. There is a pond-weed that has leaves below the surface, and also leaves on the surface. Those below are narrow, and those above the surface are broad.

6. This, too, may be one reason why leaves that are much cut are generally near the ground where the light may be shut off by other plants. Even in a healthy plant, the lower leaves, when shaded by the later leaves, tend to dwindle away. You know how the lower leaves in a wheat plant get yellow and wither even when the plant is growing strongly. This is partly because these lower leaves do not get enough of light and air.

7. **How the leaves differ on the same plant.** Again, look at a Virginia creeper and you will find that the larger leaves are outside in the full light, while the smaller leaves are in the shade. In the Japanese ivy creeper there is a difference not only in size but in shape. There is no chance about all this difference of size or shape. Pluck a leaf from an elm tree, and try to get another to match it exactly. You notice that the one half of the blade of each leaf is smaller than the other half (fig. 56). Stand

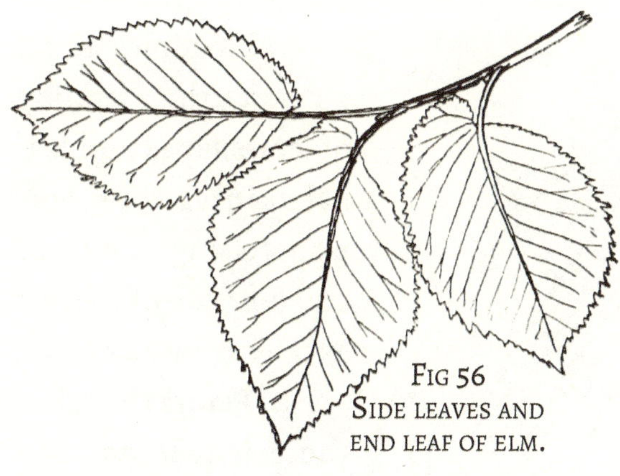

Fig 56
Side leaves and
end leaf of elm.

below an elm tree and watch how the leaves hang, and try to see how this strange shape helps the leaves to do the best they can for themselves, without cutting off the light from the other leaves. Find out also why the end leaf in an elm-twig is more regular in shape than the others.

**8. The original home of the tree must be considered.** We see, then, that nearly all the differences in the shapes of leaves are caused by the eagerness of the plant to get as much sunlight as possible; and that we can often, while standing before a tree, see how the shape or position of its leaves helps it in this way. But not always; for we do not know enough of the kind of life that the tree had to live when, in the old days, it was finding out the kind of leaf that would suit it best. The umbrella tree throws up a very high bare stem and an umbrella-shaped crown of leaves on the top. When placed by itself on a lawn, there seems to be a great waste of bare stem; but when we see the tree in the dense forest of Queensland where it is native, we understand how beautifully it is adapted to its home. And so with a hundred other trees that have been taken from their native haunts and placed in our gardens[26].

26      The way in which leaves are folded in the bud helps to determine shape; but this is a study for senior students.

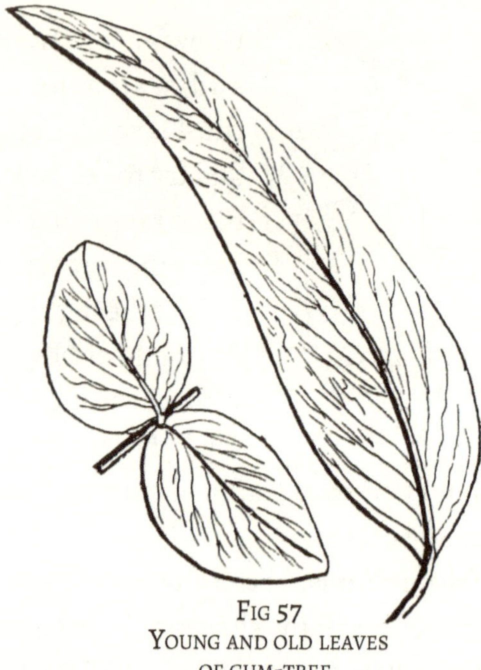
FIG 57
YOUNG AND OLD LEAVES
OF GUM-TREE.

9. Sometimes we get a clue to the meaning of leaf-shapes and leaf habits in watching how plants change the shape and position of the leaf as they grow older.

10. **Plants that alter their leaves as they grow older.** You must have noticed that a young gum-tree often has round or oval leaves, while the same tree later on has long narrow leaves. In the young blue-gum the leaves are opposite, while on the old tree the leaves hang singly (fig. 57). The young leaf, too, often holds its face to the sky, while the older leaf hangs down with its edge to the light. Here, too, let us make a guess. When the gum-tree is young, it is often struggling with other trees and shrubs as to which shall first get up into the free air and light. At this time it needs all the food and light that it can gather, and so throws out many leaves, and each leaf with its face full to the sun. When the tree has succeeded in this fight, and has got away up out of the scrub into the free air, the sun is then too strong for it, and the leaf begins to get narrower, and no longer gives its full face to the light. The leaf is now sickle-shaped; and you will notice that the longer edge is almost always turned towards the outside, where the leaf gets the most light

and air. That the early leaves are opposite need not surprise us; for the seed-leaves are always opposite, and we can trace the gradual change from opposite to alternate leaves in many plants.

11. **The first leaves of the blackwood tree.** Have you ever noticed the strange difference between the first leaves of a blackwood tree and the later leaves (fig. 58)? At first, the leaves are the usual feathery leaflets of the acacia. This feathery-form of acacia-leaf is well known to you in the common wattle and in the silver wattle. But, after the first leaf or two, the leaf-stalk begins to broaden, and then, perhaps, you find a leaf-stalk with no leaf at all on it. The feathery leaflets grow fewer and fewer as we go up, until we rarely have anything but the flattened leaf-stalks. Here, then, is a tree that has found that a green, broad leaf-stalk can do its work better than a feathery leaf. On many acacias, this green flattened leaf-stalk is so like a gum tree leaf that you may take it at first sight for a true leaf. Compare it with a gum tree leaf, and you will see, at once, that it is not an ordinary leaf. Look carefully also at a full-grown blackwood tree, and you will sometimes see, even among the higher branches, a leaf-

Fig 58

Blackwood (Lightwood). The lowest branch shows the usual acacia leaf; the third branch shows the leaf stalk beginning to flatten; the third branch shows the flattened leaf stalk taking the place of a leaf.

stalk with the true acacia leaflets on it. This shows, does it not, that what looks like a leaf is really a leaf-stalk?

12. **How sap-flow shapes the leaf.** Can you guess why the higher leaves of the ivy (fig. 59) are quite different in shape from the ordinary leaves (fig. 60)? Why is the lower leaf lobed while the upper leaf is entire? If you watch the growth of an ivy plant, you will find that it is when the growth is going on at its fastest that the lobed leaves are made. Think of the strong rush of sap up the chief ribs, and you will see that the leaf is likely to grow faster towards the points c, d, and g, than at the points n, k, m, o. Later on, when the rush of sap is not so strong, no part of the edge is pushed out more than another, and so we have the shape shown in the upper leaf. This, remember, is only a guess; but there are many other facts to support it. Examine the toothed and the entire leaves of the honeysuckle, and look at the strongest and weakest leaves of the morning glory, convolvulus, and of the bramble. You see, then, that there is still much to find out as to the cause for the shapes of leaves, but the main fact is clear: the leaves seek air and light, and it is this that fixes shape and size and position.

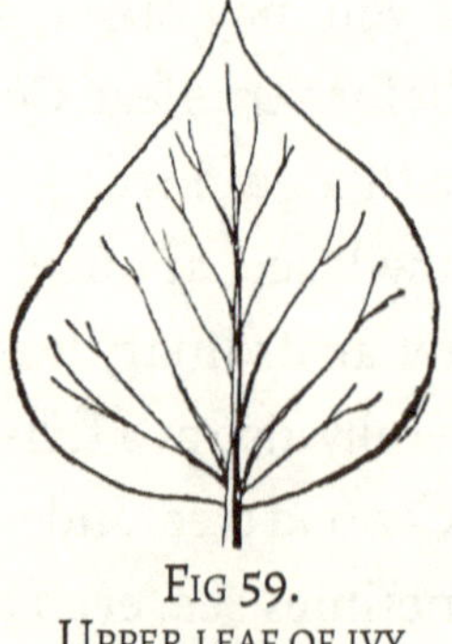

Fig 59.
UPPER LEAF OF IVY
(AN ENTIRE LEAF).

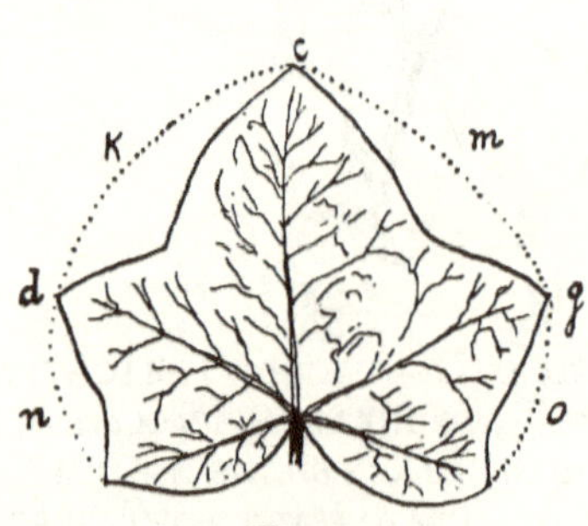

Fig 60
LOWER LEAF OF IVY.

13. **Leaves that catch flies.** To the root-food and the air-food, some plants, like the sundew, add food got by catching flies; and in these cases, the form of the leaf is altered for this purpose. The leaves bear hairs with sticky blobs of "dew" that catch insects. At the touch of a fly, the sticky dew increases, and the hairs curve over the insect. When the leaf has eaten all the soft parts of the fly, the hard parts are pushed off the leaf. Pull up a sundew, and you will find that it has few feeding roots for its size (fig. 61). Now, nitrogen is an important food, and in the ordinary plant can be got only from the root. The sundew makes up for its poor root by adding nitrogen in the form of flies. Australia is probably richer in sundews than any other land. For this reason, and on account of the beauty and interest of the plant, the sundews should be carefully studied.

Fig 61
Whittaker's sundew
(after von Mueller).

Questions and Exercises.

(1) If the outer edge of it hanging gum tree leaf grows faster than the inner edge, what must be the effect on the shape of the leaf?

(2) Compare the shape of the opposite leaflets of the Japanese anemone with the shape of the end leaflet. Compare elm leaves.

(3) Sow thickly some seed, and allow the seedlings to grow up without thinning. This will show how crowded plants suffer in the struggle to get light and air.

(4) One or two Cape weeds should be kept under observation, in early spring, to see how they smother the smaller plants.

(5) Scholars living near the sea should note the fleshiness of many of the coast-plants as compared with similar inland plants.

(6) The hairs of the sundew will not close upon sand or other things that the leaf cannot eat. Test one or two plants.

(7) Name any of the acacias that have flattened leaf-stalks instead of leaves.

**Composition Exercise.** Write the story of a guni tree, from the time when it rises out of the ground to the time when it rises high above the scrub.

**Drawing Exercise.** Draw side by side (*a*) young and old leaves of a gum tree; (*b*) the lower and upper leaves of an ivy plant.

# XIV

# How Leaves Protect Themselves

1. Very wonderful are the plans by which leaves are protected from cold, from heat, and from animals.

2. **How leaves are protected from cold.** Have you ever noticed the blackened leaves on a pittosporum hedge after a frosty night in spring? All tender leaves are easily hurt on a clear, cold night, when there are no clouds to act as blankets to the earth and to the life upon it. During the day, a leaf is spread out with its face to the sky. If tender leaves like those of the clover were kept in this position at night, they would soon lose all their heat and be in danger of frost-bite. Some leaves, therefore, tuck themselves up snugly for the night.

3. Watch a clover plant, and you will see how it is done. By day, the clover spreads out its three pretty leaflets to the sun (fig. 62). At nightfall, the two opposite leaflets fall down and come close together; and then the third leaflet bends gradually over until it forms a roof to cover the other two! It is the upper side of the leaf that most needs protection from

Fig 62
CLOVER LEAFLETS BY
DAY AND NIGHT.

99

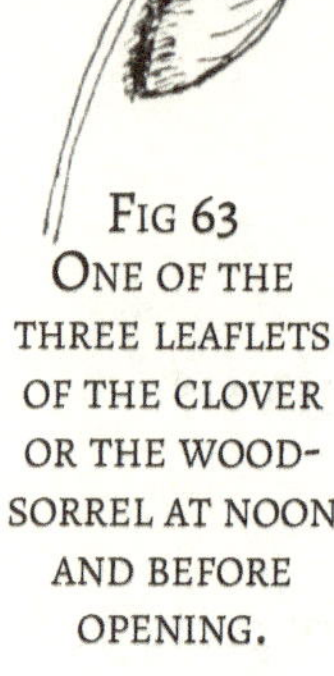

Fig 63
One of the three leaflets of the clover or the wood-sorrel at noon and before opening.

cold, and, by this plan, all the upper sides are covered[27]. You can now look for yourselves at the many plans for keeping the cold from leaves when they are just leaving the bud. Fig. 63 will show you one plan, but there are many others. Look at the top of a gum sapling and try to find how the tender young leaves are guarded from cold. Gum leaves hang downwards: why do the baby-leaves point upwards? The plans for guarding leaves against heat are chiefly of two kinds: plans for storing up water, and plans for checking the loss of it.

5. **Leaves that store water.** Look at the weed called portulaca or purslane, which over-runs our gardens in the summer, and you will see that the leaf is thick and fleshy, and full of water. Here is a plant that revels in the hottest sunshine. Then there are the stone-crops and the morning flowers that make so many dry places gay with their star-like flowers. In these, and in many other plants, the fleshy stem

Fig 64
Morning flower, showing fleshy leaves.

27     On Mt. Kosciusko, and other high points, plants are often hairier than the same plants on the plains, in order to protect them from the mountain cold.

works like the leaf in the task of getting food from the air. Then there are the thick-leaved cactuses that we have brought from hot desert lands into our gardens.

6. **Leaves that check the loss of water.** A thin, soft leaf would be burned up at once in the desert, and so the cactus has a hard skin to keep the water from escaping quickly from its thick leaves. Other desert plants check the escape of water by having their leaves tough and narrow, or curled under at the edge; others, again, have salt in the sap, and this, too, prevents the moisture from escaping quickly. A thick coat of hairs is often used, especially on the underside of the leaf, to check evaporation. It was only the other day that it was found out that heat does not easily pass through a spray of perfume; but, for ages, some of the plants of hot lands have been softening the effect of the sun's rays by throwing off perfume from their leaves. This may give to you a new view of the scents that come from the oil in the leaves of our gum trees.

7. **How leaves are guarded against animals.** Some leaves guard themselves against animals by keeping flat on the ground; others are passed over because they have a taste that the animals do not like; while others again, like the gorse, lift themselves boldly up and defy the animals to touch them.

8. **Plants that lie flat on the ground.** How cleverly the dandelion flattens itself out on the ground! Even when its time of flowering comes, and it must hoist up its flower, it waits till it is quite ready to open. Then up it goes, to get the help of the sun and the wind and the bees. When the pollen has done its work, down the flower falls again to be out of danger while it is ripening the seed. As soon as it is ready to open out into the

FIG 65

LEAVES OF BLUE GUM SHOWING THE OIL-DOTS (AFTER VON MUELLER).

beautiful seed-balloon, the stalk rises again, lengthening itself so as to be clear of the grass, and the wind whisks away the winged seed! How beautifully it is all planned! Even should the leaves chance to be eaten, the plant is not killed. Fresh leaves come from the thick tap-root. In this way, or in similar ways, the plants of the field and of the roadside live and thrive. They can travel better than the fine flowers of the garden, and many of them can be found all over the world.

FIG 66
SCOTCH THISTLE.

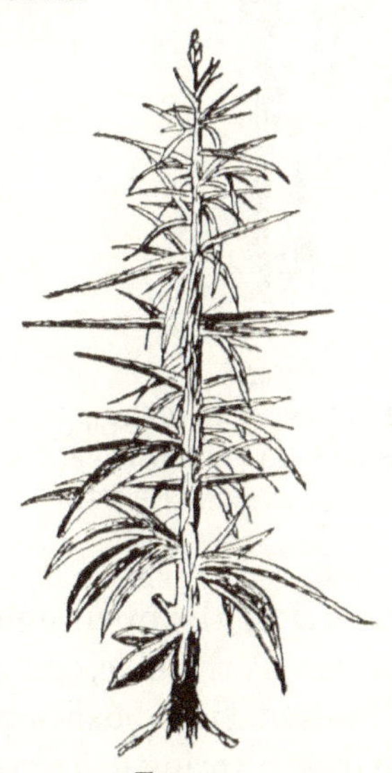

FIG 67
GORSE SEEDLING, SHOWING HOW
THE SOFT THREE-LOBED LEAF
GRADUALLY TURNS INTO A SPINE.

9. **Plants guarded by thorns and spines.** In passing today through a close-cropped field, I noticed that all the plants had been eaten close to the ground except three—a gorse bush, a Scotch thistle, and a sow-thistle. The soft sow-thistle was growing up boldly through the leaves of the great Scotch thistle. Many a cow had looked longingly at it but did not dare to touch it.

Fig 68.
THE COMMON RIB-GRASS,
WHICH LIES FLAT WHEN THERE
IS DANGER OF IT BEING CROPPED.

10. Hairs are often so thick or so stiff that they help to keep off animals. In a few cases, too, the hairs sting, as in the nettle. The soft noses of cattle are easily hurt. Look through a lens at a nettle-hair. It consists of a tiny flask of stinging fluid, and this flask ends in a very delicate sharp point. If you snip off a little piece of leaf or stem with a pair of scissors, and hold it on a pin, you can look at the "sting" comfortably.

## Questions and Exercises.

(1) Find out how the wood-sorrel protects its three leaflets from the night cold.

(2) How do the opening leaves of the following plants guard against cold? Periwinkle, common garden pea, castor-oil plant, ferns.

(3) Fires of damp bushes causing much smoke are sometimes lit in orchards in spring to keep off frost. Explain.

(4) One sometimes sees in spring a light covering of straw on potato plants. How does this help the plants?

(5) Name any plants in your district that stand drought well, giving reasons.

(6) The leaves of the holly near the ground have prickles, but those higher up have none. Explain.

(7) The shining dots that you see in a gum tree leaf when the leaf is held up to the light are scent-cells. Can you tell of any way in which this scent may be of use to the leaves? Name any other plants in your district that have scented leaves.

(8) Study the summer weed called wire-weed, and find out why it

can grow on bare, dry patches where little else can grow. If possible, take up the whole root.

(9) Study the flat weed (mock dandelion). In what points are its habits similar to those of the dandelion, and in what different? Each head of the dandelion lies down between flower-time and balloon-time. Why is the habit of the flat-weed different?

(10) How does the Bathurst burr protect itself?

(11) Show how man copied Nature in choosing his hedge-plants. Name some good hedge-plants.

(12) Where are thorns placed in (*a*) the rose, (*b*) the hawthorn, (*c*) the prickly acacia?

(13) Make a list of some of the pasture-plants of your district that cattle will not eat.

(14) The oleander is a hot-climate shrub. How does it protect its leaves from the direct rays of the sun? Compare the gum tree leaves.

(15) How is it that a nettle is harmless when grasped quickly and strongly?

(16) The young shoots of some of our mountain plants are regularly shortened by cutting winds. In spite of this, these plants thrive. Compare grasses that have been cropped by animals for ages.

(17) Watch the narrow-leaved plantain (rib grass) in a close-cropped field, and then compare with one in some corner where it is free to grow up.

**Composition Exercise.**

Tell how the gorse has managed to thrive in spite of many enemies, or the dandelion, the plantain, the flat weed, or any other roadside weed.

**Drawing Exercise.**

(1) Draw a clover leaf as it looks (*a*) before opening out; (*b*) by day; (*c*) at nightfall.

(2) Draw a branch of any prickly plant—Bathurst burr, thistle, furze, &c.

XV.

# The Flower

PART I

WHAT IS A FLOWER?

1. **What is a flower? A seed-maker.** We have seen how hard the plant works; how root and stem and leaves are as busy as the day is long. To what end is all this work? To make a flower, you say. Now, I know that you mean by a flower the beautiful blossoms of the violet-plant, the rose bush, the pansy, and many others. But some, nay most plants, have no beautiful blooms of this kind. They **flower** as all plants do; but they do it in a way that never catches the eye.

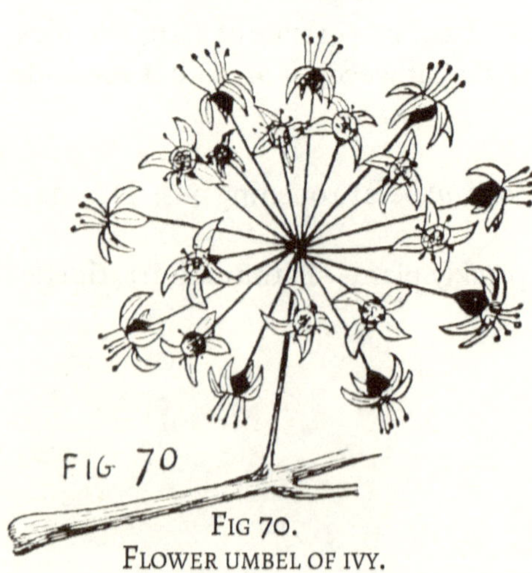


FIG 70.
FLOWER UMBEL OF IVY.

2. **Is a flower always coloured?** How many people notice the flower of the ivy? Not many; and yet the ivy has a flower so cleverly planned that it never fails to get what most flowers want to get—plenty of insect visitors. Through my window I can see a score of flies, big and lit-

106

tle, blue and black, sipping the honey on the ivy-flowers that grow on the fence. Out and in the flies go; thinking only of the honey, but, all the time, carrying the pollen on their backs from one flower to another. A large fly that looks like a bee, but is not a bee, is making sudden dashes here and there about the garden, when, all at once, it stops and settles on the ivy-blossom. Within five minutes, I count ten other flies that do the same thing. One would think that there was some bad meat on the fence to draw all these flies; for they are flesh-flies, every one. Ah! Now we have hit it! The ivy-blossom has a smell like meat that has gone bad—not pleasant to you, but a smell that draws the flesh-flies from far and wide.

3. So, then, "you exclaim, a flower is a part of the plant meant to attract insects?" Well, you are getting near to the secret; you are "burning," as we say in the parlour game; but you are not quite right yet.

4. **Is a flower always scented?** Let us stroll out into a field of wheat in the spring-time and seek the secret there. The graceful, rustling heads welcome us, but not by gay colour. By scent, then? No, not by scent. There is nothing to catch the eye of that bee that is humming past; and there is no smell to draw the flies. You may watch for a long October day, and never see a bee nor a fly go near to a wheat-flower. No insect comes, and yet all goes well with the wheat-plant, and the beautiful heads whisper as they bend to the spring breeze. See how the pollen is blown about as the wind freshens! Can that be the secret? Does the wheat-flower use the wind to bear its pollen? Does the wind take the place of insects? Yes, that is the secret of the

wheat-flower, and it is the secret of all the grasses and reeds and of many trees.

5. "So, then," you say, "the flower is something that requires to scatter its pollen, and it matters little whether an insect carries it or the wind carries it?" Now you are nearer still to the secret. A flower must scatter the golden dust so that it may fall on its own seed-case or on the seed-case of another flower of the same kind; for you must know that no flower can make seed unless the pollen falls on it.

6. **The purpose of a flower.** Then you try once more: "Is a flower, then, a part of the plant that makes pollen in order to make seed?" Yes, now we have it. The purpose of the flower is to make seed. It may have no colour and no scent and yet be a flower if it can only make seed.

7. If a plant could live for itself alone, what would become of next year's crop of plants? The plant's time comes to wither and die; and it makes seed so that, next year, the fields and gardens may be as beautiful as they are today. Yes, that is the flower's secret: to pass on its life to its children.

8. Where are the plants of last year? The wheat-plants of last spring have gone, and even the stubble has been turned over by the plough; but the wheat-plants of next spring sleep safely in the golden grain that the farmer has stored away for seed. Your poppies have long since withered away—flowers and leaves and root—but next year's poppies lie safely hidden in the little packet of seed which you took from the poppy-flowers.

9. **Many are the plans of the flowers for making seed.** Already you have seen that the various plants have various ways of making seed. Some use bright colours to help them; others have

no colour at all. Some make use of scent; others are scentless. Some use insects as carriers of the pollen; others use birds, and still others use the wind. Some flowers, again, like chickweed, use neither insects nor the wind, because they are able to dust their own seed-case with their own pollen. Most of the plants with green flowers or with very small coloured flowers use their own pollen.

10. There are a hundred plans; but the plan we shall look at first is that of the plants that have gay flowers to attract pollen-carriers. We shall see how one of these gay flowers is built up, and how all the parts work to one end—the **making of seed.**

Questions.

(1) Name some plants that flower without gay colour.

(2) Name some flowers that attract insects by scent.

(3) Name some plants or trees that use the wind to carry their pollen.

(4) Name some flowers that use bees to carry their pollen.

(5) Can you name any plants (mostly weeds) that seem to have no need of insects nor of the wind?

*N.B.*—The flowers in these cases are generally very small and often green.

**Composition Exercise.**

Watch carefully the visits of bees or other insects to a flower or bed of flowers, and write an account of what you see.

**Drawing Exercise.**

Make a drawing of (*a*) an ivy flower umbel; (*b*) a single ivy-flower.

XVI.

# The Flower

<u>PART II</u>

THE PARTS OF A FLOWER.

1. **The scarlet geranium.** The scarlet geranium is to be found in almost every garden from the Murray to the sea, and it is in flower during most months of the year. We shall, therefore, find out how a flower is built up by taking to pieces a scarlet geranium.

2. **The flower-stalk.** First of all, we notice the long stout flower-stalk that pushes the flower-cluster well above the green leaves. We can guess at once from this long stalk that the flower needs the help of bees or flies. Whenever a flower is thrust high into the air, we know that this is done either to catch the eyes of passing insects, or in order that its pollen or its seed may be more easily scattered.

3. **Why is the flower-stalk hairy?** The flower-stalk is hairy, and many of the longer hairs point downwards. The downward-pointing hairs make it harder for small insects to climb up to the flower. But, does not the flower wish the insects to come to it? Yes, but not any insect. Bees and large flies are welcome, because these go in at the front door and help to scatter the pollen. But ants and other small insects often creep into the

110

honey-tube without touching the pollen-dust at all. Even if an ant be touched, the pollen does not stick on its smooth body, and so the ant cannot carry pollen to another flower. These honey-thieves take something from the flower and give nothing in return. The honey is meant as a fee to the large flying insects that can do work for the flower. Look now at the hairs on the leaf-stalks of the plant, and you will see that few of them point downwards; for the leaves do not need to be guarded like the flowers.

4. The green sheath enclosing the flower-cluster. At the end of the flower-stalk is a green sheath, within which is packed a bunch of flowers. Was ever packing so close and neat! The sheath is to keep the flower-buds warm, and also to keep moths and flies from laying their eggs in the flowers. You may have found a rosebud with a grub inside.

5. When the green sheath is burst open by the swelling buds, out comes a flower on a long stalklet, and then another and another, until the cluster of flowers looks like a scarlet umbrella bending over the flower-buds that are still unopened[28]. By this beautiful plan, the young tender flower-buds are protected from the night cold by the older flowers. Look at the colour of a flower-bud that is just breaking through the green, and compare it with the colour of the fully opened flowers. If you hold up to the sunlight a bud half-open, you will see that there is a gleam of golden dust among the scarlet. Note also that each stalklet looks like two stems pinned together. We shall see presently the meaning of this.

6. **The calyx.** The stalklet ends in a little green cup (*calyx*),

28     A cluster of this kind is called a umbel (L. *umbra*, shade.)

which holds together the five scarlet petals. This cup also is cut into five parts (*sepals*), and you will notice that the sepals are not all of the same size. If you look at one of the flower-buds that has not yet begun to open, you will see that it is completely covered by the calyx. The calyx, therefore, is meant to protect the flower-bud. It is meant to do for a single flower what the green sheath did for the whole cluster of flowers. How snug the flower was, hid in its little cloak, and that little cloak hid in another great one... The calyx, then, is meant to shield the flower when it is a bud, and to support it when it has opened out into a flower.

7. **The corolla.** And now we come to the five beautiful leaves called petals, that make up the flower's little crown (*corolla*). You notice that two of these petals are smaller than the rest, and that they are more deeply grooved than the larger petals. Look at the veins on the undersides of all the petals. The other three larger petals overlap a good deal; the two smaller do not overlap much, but, in the fully opened flower, are set almost edge to edge.

8. **The honey-tube.** Pull off now all the sepals except the largest, and all the petals. Take then your lens and see what lies hid at the base of the largest sepal. You see a hole leading down into the stalklet. Probe it with a pin, and you find that it goes down a long way. Here then

Fig 71
THE PETALS OF THE SCARLET GERANIUM.

is a tube. And now squeeze the tube gently between finger and thumb, and you will see that a fluid rises to the mouth of the tube. Put this to your tongue. It is sweet! We have found the honey-store! Also, we have found out the meaning of the ridge on the stem that made it look like a double stem. The ridge is the honey-tube.

9. **The path to the honey**. And now take another full flower, and see how the insect reaches this honey. The insect will alight on the largest of the petals. This large petal makes a kind of front step, and is strong enough with the help of the two other large petals to bear a large insect's weight. The insect will then push its head down the little opening at the base of the two smallest petals. As these petals meet only edge to edge, they will easily open to make room for the head of the insect. Now the largest sepal is always at the back of these two smallest petals; and we saw that the honey-tube is at the base of this large sepal. Notice also that the swellings at the base of the two small petals guide the eye at once to the door of the honey-tube. The insect, there-fore, loses no time in finding the honey-store. It cannot push its head into the honey-tube, but its sucker is long enough to reach into the tube. In the next chapter we shall see what the flower owes to these honey-sucking insects.

<u>Questions and Exercises:</u>

(1) Before eating a strawberry you remove a little ring of leaves attached to the fruit. What is this?

(2) Why are the unopened flower-buds in a geranium cluster curved round towards the flower-stalk?

(3) What is the colour of the geranium flower when just breaking through the calyx, and of the flower when fully opened?

(4) The calyx of a poppy falls off as soon as the flower opens. Compare with this the calyx of geranium and mallow weed.

(5) In a fuchsia the corolla is coloured. Can you see why the calyx also is coloured?

(6) Is the calyx green or coloured in the nasturtium, violet, larkspur, oleander, native fuchsia (correa)?

(7) In the geranium the calyx supports the corolla. How does the calyx of the rose behave?

(8) In the geranium all the calyx remains after the flower opens. Does all the calyx of a gumtree flower remain?

(9) In the geranium the corolla is made up of petals that can be pulled out one by one. Explain the difference in honeysuckle, primrose, Canterbury bell.

(10) The calyx in the geranium has only one whorl (ring) of sepals. How is it with the strawberry and the mallow weed?

(11) Some plants are hairy or sticky just below the flower to keep off small insects. Try to find examples.

**Composition Exercise**. Place before you all the parts of a geranium flower that has been pulled apart, and tell how you could put them together again so as to make a complete flower. Begin with the stalklet of a single flower. Be careful to build up the flower so that an insect may be able easily to reach the honey-tube.

**Drawing Exercise**: (*a*) Draw the five petals of a geranium flower, showing how they differ in size. (*b*) Draw two or three rose sepals, showing how they differ in shape.

XVII.

# The Flower

<u>PART III</u>

THE PARTS OF A FLOWER (continued).

1. We have looked at the calyx of the scarlet geranium, and we have seen how the calyx protects the flower when it is young. We have looked also at the corolla whose gay colour calls out to passing insects: "Here is pollen; come and eat; here is honey; come and sip!"

2. We have now to look at the stamens, the parts of the flower that bear the pollen-cases. Take a flower that is only half-open, and, with the help of a pin, turn back the sepals, and hold them between finger and thumb. Then, still using the pin, take off very gently the outside small petal. You can easily find this outside petal because it is always opposite to the largest sepal. Then take off the other small petal, and then the three largest petals. Notice, as you do this, how beautifully the petals are folded. You see now ten small red stalks, some of which end in red pollen-cases. The stalks are the **stamens**, and the pollen-cases are called **anthers**. You will see that there are no pollen-cases on three of the stamens; and we guess from this that the flower has learned to get on with fewer anthers than it needed at some far-past time.

115

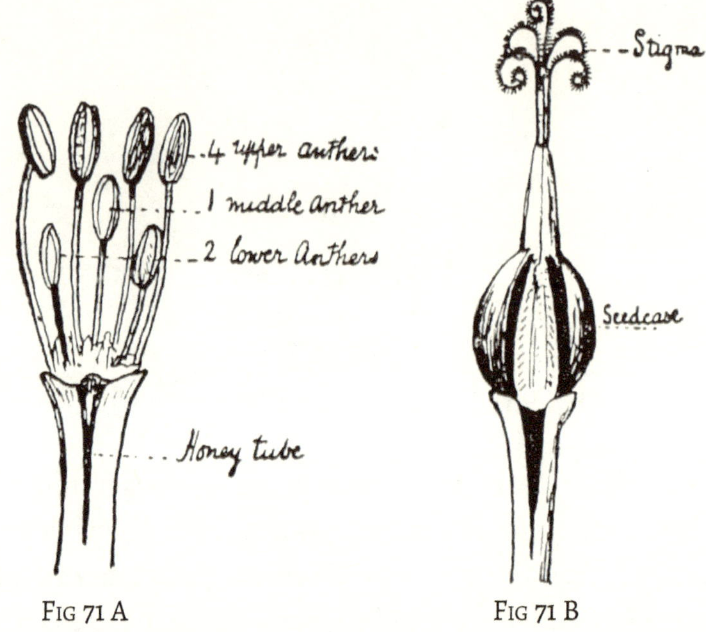



FIG 71 A          FIG 71 B

FIG 71 A AND B. THE ANTHERS AND PISTIL OF THE SCARLET GERANIUM.

3. **How the stamens differ.** Notice that two of the stamens are shorter than the others; that these two short stamens always have pollen-cases; and that they are always opposite to the honey-tube. What does this mean? It means that when the insect pushes its sucker down into the honey-tube it cannot help touching the pollen-cases on these two short stamens. It may escape the pollen on the tall stamens, but not the pollen on these short stamens. Nor is this all. The third anther, as we go up, is midway between the short stamens and the long ones, and thus the flower has three chances of dusting the insect with pollen; first, with the tallest anthers, second, with the middle anther, and third with the lowest anthers. Even now we have not seen the whole of the plan for dusting the insect with pollen; for if you take a riper flower that has the pollen-cases open, you will

see that the pollen is always shed towards the honey-path. You will see this most clearly in an anther just beginning to split. Notice that the pollen bursting from the middle anther almost blocks the way to the honey. You will have noticed, while pulling the flower to pieces, that the anthers fall off unless you do the work very gently. The lowest anthers hold on better than the others. This is important because these anthers are the ones most likely to touch the insect.

4. **The pistil.** If now you remove the ten stamens with your pin, you will see that a red-stalked body is left. This is the **pistil**. It is stouter than a stamen, and it shows signs of dividing at the top. This top of the pistil is called the **stigma**. No seed can be made unless the pollen-dust falls on the stigma.

5. **The seed-case**. Take now a riper flower and remove the sepals, petals, and stamens. The pistil is now a pretty object. It has split at the top into five ends that curve gracefully outwards. At the foot of the red pistil is a hairy, green body. This is the seed-case. In this are the tiny bodies that will swell into full seeds if the top of the pistil, the stigma, can catch some pollen.

6. You notice that the seed-case is of two parts, the bottom part being broader than the top part. It is in the bottom part that the seeds lie, and already you can see them swelling. With the help of your lens, you will find that there are five seeds. Do you see now why the pistil divides, at the stigma, into five parts? The truth is that the red pistil-stalk is made up of five pistil-stalks, each of which leads down to one of the five seeds.

7. **How the seed is thrown off.** Take now a flower in the seeding stage, but not quite ripe. At this stage it looks like the long tapering bill of a stork. The hairy, green body which formed

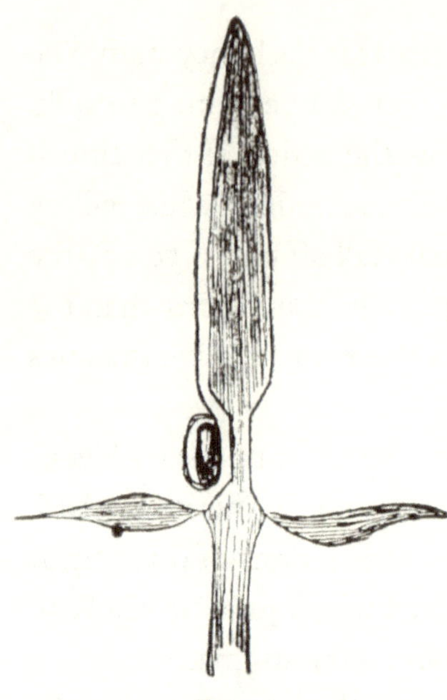

FIG 72
WILD GERANIUM ABOUT TO THROW
ITS LAST SEED. SEE ALSO FIG. 94.

the upper part of the seed-case has now lengthened into a long column marked by five red lines. You guess at once that these five red lines run down to the five seed-cases. Looking now at a riper flower, you can clearly see that this is correct. Each red line has become a long, narrow stalk, which is ready to jerk its seed away from the column. When quite ripe, these stalks become elastic and curl up suddenly so that the seed in the seed-case is thrown into the air. This is one of a thousand plans that plants have for scattering their seed.

8. **The five-fold flowers**. We have now seen that the flower is made up of four separate rings or whorls: the first ring being the sepals, the second the petals, the third the stamens, and the fourth the pistil. No doubt you have noticed that the numbers in three of the rings go by **fives**; and we may suppose that the ten stamens were, in earlier times, in two rows of five each. You must not suppose that in all flowers the rings go by fives. In some they go by threes; but the five-fold plan is the one that we find in most of our familiar flowers. With a few exceptions, like the wall-flower, the plants that have two seed-leaves have the five-fold plan. Plants that grow from seeds with one seed-leaf have their flowers built upon a **three-fold plan**.

Questions and Exercises:

(1) Look at various kinds of flowers, and note that (*a*) plants with leaves that have a network of veins have flowers that are nearly all on the **five-fold** plan; (*b*) plants that have leaves with parallel veins have flowers that are on the **three-fold** plan.

(2) Pollen is generally yellow. What is the colour of the pollen in the geranium, and in the petunia? Can you name any other flower that has pollen of unusual colour?

(3) The corolla of the geranium has five petals. How many have wall-flowers and poppies?

(4) How many stamens have salvia, veronica, wall-flower, lark-spur, foxglove?

**Composition Exercise**: Tell how the geranium flower is planned so that the insect cannot reach the honey without getting dusted with pollen.

**Drawing Exercise:**

(1) Draw a single geranium flower: (*a*) entire; (*b*) with all the parts removed except the stamens and pistil; (*c*) with only the pistil (with divided stigma) left.

(2) Draw the ripe geranium seed-case.

XVIII.

# The Flower

<u>PART IV</u>
THE GERANIUM'S DEBT TO INSECTS

1. I am now ready to reply to the question which you have been waiting to ask: Why was the stigma of the geranium so late in opening? Why was the pollen nearly all shed before the stigma was ready to receive it? Because, I reply, the flower is planned so as to be able to send its pollen to other geranium flowers, and, in return, to receive their pollen. The geranium is planned so as to avoid dusting its stigma with its own pollen.

2. All flowers are not like the geranium in this. Many flowers, nay, most flowers, use their own pollen for making seed; but most of the finest flowers send away their pollen to other plants, and get pollen from them in return.

3. And now you have another question ready: Why can't a flower be a fine flower if it uses its own pollen for making seed?

4. **Mixed races in men and flowers.** Well, I reply, you have seen the same thing in your History lessons. The finest races in the world's history are those that have not kept to themselves, but have mixed their blood with that of other races. How many kinds of man have gone to the making of an Englishman? If the English had been able to keep themselves to themselves in their

120

little island, would they have been great today? Races that do not easily mix with other races remain in the background; just as flowers that cannot be crossed easily with others are likely to remain among the weeds. If I told you all that the garden owes to the mixture of flowers, I should fill up many chapters; and so let me show you instead what our geranium flower has gained by giving and receiving pollen.

5. **The long flower-stalk.** First of all, our geranium may owe its long flower-stalk to this, because a flower that uses its own pollen has no need to get high up in the air to be seen by bees and flies. The flowers that use their own pollen are often so low down, or so much hid among the green leaves, that it is hard to see them. Many a man never notices the flowers of the groundsel or of the wire-weed that runs along close to the ground.

6. **The gay colour.** Then the geranium owes its beautiful scarlet petals to the visits of insects. Flowers that use their own pollen have generally small, dull-looking flowers, and often no colour at all. The force which, in our garden flowers, goes to the making of large flower-stalks and large gay petals is, in these weeds, spent in stems and leaves and seeds; and this is one reason why the weeds can so quickly overrun a garden.

7. But in our geranium, not only are the petals coloured but also the stamens, and the pollen, and the pistil. Scarlet is a colour easily seen by insects that fly in the daytime; but it would not be easily seen at night; and so we find that flowers that need the visits of night insects never have red flowers. They have generally pale yellow or white colours that can be seen readily in the dark.

8. **The door-step.** And not only does our geranium draw the

flies by gay petals, but these petals are built so as to suit the insects in every way. Look at the flower as it sits on the plant, and you will see that one of the petals is a front door-step for the insects to alight on. This petal is a large one, and it is also supported by the next two petals, so that it is strong enough to bear the weight of a large insect. And now the bee is ready to thrust its head into the honey-track, if it can find it. Nothing easier!

9. **Guides to the honey-tube.** Right in front of the bee are the two smallest petals, and on these petals are honey-guides. Yes, it is true! The flower has its finger-posts to show the way to the honey! Grooves are on the small petals, and these grooves lead to one place—a little hole. Follow up this track, and you will come to the honey-tube. The insect knows it, and loses not a second in finding the hole and in thrusting in its sucker. Meantime, the upper stamens are dusting the breast of the insect with pollen, and the lower stamens are dusting its head and sucker; so that when it flies to a riper flower that has the stigma open, the dust is sure to fall where it is wanted.

10. **The honey-tube**. And then there is the honey-tube itself. But for the insects, there would have been no honey-tube. We know this because flowers that have never had their pollen carried by insects have no honey.

11. Even now we have not got to the end of the list of the things the geranium owes to the insects. We have still to add the downward-pointing hairs of the flower-stalk, which keep small honey thieves from creeping up. No insects, no honey; no honey, no downward-pointing hairs!

12. **Why does the scarlet geranium make so little seed?** And now we come to a difficulty. I have just been looking for ripe

seed-cases; and out of forty flowers I have found only four that have succeeded in getting ripe seed. Four out of forty! Well, you must remember that the scarlet geranium did not learn its ways in a garden. If you want merely to see a lion, you go to the Zoological Gardens; but if you want to know all about a lion, you must go to the wilds of Africa, where the lion is at home. In the same way, to know the scarlet geranium[29] fully, you must go to South Africa, where it is native. Only there can we see how well it is planned to make seed with the help of insects. If we carry it away from its native fields to a garden; if we take it away from Africa to Australia; if we take away the flower without the insect which is its friend, we cannot expect to see all its plans in full working order.

13. Here again the weeds that use their own pollen have a great advantage over the finer flowers; and this is one reason why weeds like chickweed, groundsel, sow thistle, and black nightshade are to be found thriving in all parts of the world. Out of 40,000 flowers on an Australian orchid, only one had a seed-pod. This was because the insect friend was absent. But most weeds have no need of insects for dusting their flowers with pollen. But you must not think that all the gay flowers are seedless when insects do not visit them. Some, indeed, like aconite and many of the orchids, are able to make little or no seed without the help of insects; others, like the scarlet geranium and white clover, can make a little seed without this help; others, again, like the gorse and the snapdragon, make seed quite freely even when bees do not come; and in a few cases, like the sweet pea and the common pea, the flower receives no

29    This is really a pelargonium.

insect visitors at all. The seeds of the sweet violet, too, are not produced by the violet flowers, but by green flower-buds that grow near the ground and that never open. To understand all these exceptions to the general rule, we would require to know the full story for ages back of each plant[30].

14. That, then, is one reason why the geranium has "set" so few seeds; but there is another reason. The weather has been rainy, and rainy weather not only keeps insects from flying, but often injures pollen. Do you remember the year when your pear tree bore no pears? Well, that was a year when long-continued rains came just as the pear tree was in blossom.

### Questions and Exercises:

(1) Compare the honey-store of the nasturtium with that of the scarlet geranium. How do they differ?

(2) In the nasturtium, the stamens ripen first. Later on, when the stamens have retired, the stigma opens and bends down to the very place where the anthers were. Explain the reason for this.

(3) Name the chief weeds, like groundsel, shepherd's purse, chickweed, &c., that thrive in your district. Distinguish between summer weeds and weeds that can live in any weather.

**Composition Exercise:** All our finer garden flowers owe their beauty largely to the visits of insects. Explain this.

**Drawing Exercise:** Draw the flower of the nasturtium, showing the guide-lines to the honey.

---

30      Fossil records indicate that there were no coloured petals before insects arrived in the world. It would seem, then, that some flowers, like the sweet pea, after passing through the stage of insect-partnership, have (without giving up their gay petals) fallen back on self-fertilization. Others, while still able to make use of the insects, can "set" seed without them.

XIX.

# The Flower

<u>PART V</u>

REGULAR AND IRREGULAR FLOWERS

1. **Tubular flowers**. In our scarlet geranium we found that the petals could be pulled off one by one. In many flowers, like the plumbago and honeysuckle, the petals are all joined together in a tube; and we shall call such flowers **tubular flowers**.

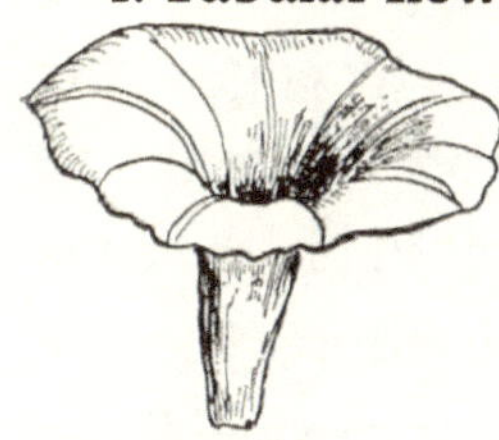

FIG 73
TUBULAR FLOWER.

2. **Regular and irregular flowers**. In our geranium, the petals are not all alike, but the difference between one petal and another is so little that few people know that the petals differ at all. But in some of the tubular flowers, like the snapdragon or the larkspur or the salvia, the tube of petals is so irregular that everyone notices it. Well, we shall call such flowers **irregular** to distinguish them from flowers like the poppy or the Canterbury bell, which are **regular** all round the corolla.

FIG 74
REGULAR FLOWER.

3. We saw that the petals of the scarlet

geranium are built to suit the visiting insect; and no doubt you have already guessed that the strange-looking petals of irregular flowers are all planned for the same purpose. We saw that the front petal of the geranium, on which the insect alights, has become larger and stronger than the other petals so as to bear the insect's weight.

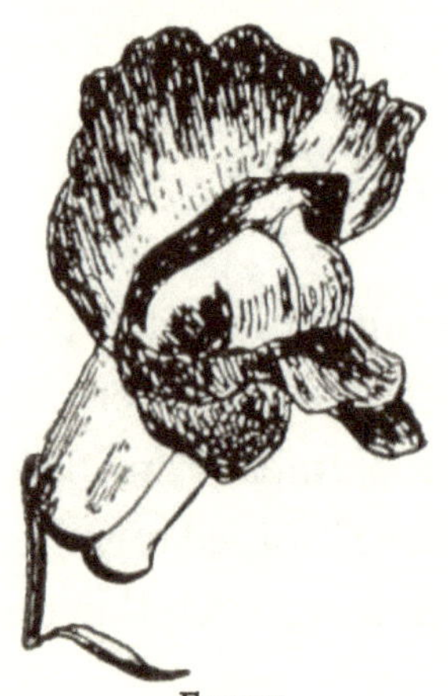

Fig 75
Irregular flower,
Snapdragon.

4. Now let us look at an **irregular flower—the snapdragon**—and see whether this gives us a clue to its curious shape. Think of a great bee, the humble bee of England, coming down heavily on the outer edge of the flower tube. Think of this going on for a thousand years! Would the edge on which the bee rested not become stronger than the opposite edge? What happens when you use your right hand more than your left hand? Why are the muscles of a blacksmith's arms "strong as iron bands"? Exactly the same rule holds in plant life. This has been actually proved by hanging weights on leaves and twigs. The fibres, which are the muscles of the leaf-stalk, become larger and stronger.

5. **How the snapdragon got its mouth.** It was probably in this way that the edge of the snapdragon flower-tube became larger and stronger; and as the edge was broadened and bent down, the tube below it was pinched in till the entrance to the flower was closed. So firmly was it closed that only the great humble-bee can force its way in. The little hive-bee tries to go in sometimes, but is hardly strong enough. Inside, as well

Fig 76
Foxglove.

as outside, the flower-tube is planned to suit this large bee. The only way in which thieves can get to the honey is by biting a hole in the bottom of the tube. Yesterday, I noticed a honey-bird busy among the flowers of a snapdragon; and when I looked closely, I found that every one of the tubes had been pierced by the bird's bill just above the honey stores!

6. **Flowers with a lip.** Many other flowers have an alighting stage like the lip of the snapdragon, and, indeed, a large family of flowers is called the Lip-flowered family. This family includes the salvias, lavender, thyme, and mint. Notice that the lip is always in front, in the part of the flower where the insect alights. Notice, too, that many irregular flowers—the snapdragon, the larkspur, the gladiolus, the foxglove—run up in spikes; and each flower is so close to the stem that the bee can visit it only from one side. The bee, therefore, has no choice as to the petals he shall alight upon; and hence, probably, the large lip. Compare such flowers with regular flowers like the poppy or the tulip, which do not grow close to the side of a spike, and you will see that there is nothing to hinder the bee from alighting on any part of the corolla. There is nothing, therefore, to cause such flowers to

grow irregular[31]. And here we have to notice a most interesting fact. Now and then, the end-flower of a spike of larkspur, foxglove, or snapdragon is quite regular in shape. Can you guess the meaning of this?

7. The various ways in which the irregular flowers are fitted for the insects that visit them are very wonderful. Each flower has its own plan, and we can look at only one or two. Let us look at the plan of this large blue garden salvia.

8. **How the salvia dusts the bee.** We note first of all that the corolla is tubular, and that the tube is divided into a lip and a hood. Next, we note how the lip has been made strong by extra cords in order to bear the weight of the bee. The hood protects the anthers and the pistil from the rain. And now we look carefully at the stamens. There are but two anthers, and these are on stamens with a peculiar arrangement of levers. We follow down the stamens, and find these levers. And now, we thrust a straw down to the tube, and find that, when it touches the levers, the anthers bend forward towards the lip. A visiting bee could not fail to receive the pollen on its back. The

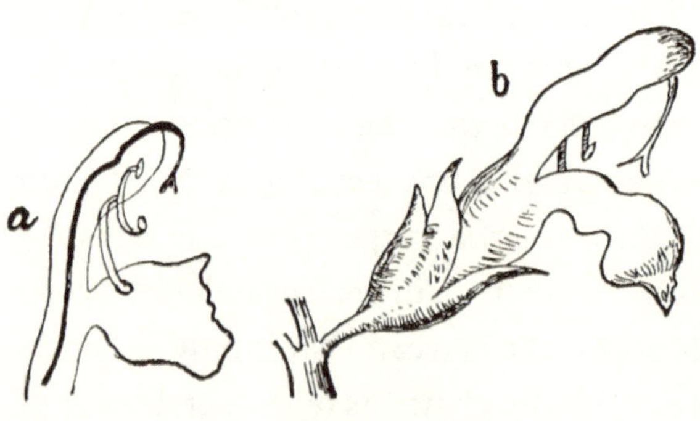


Fig 77

SALVIA: (A) A FLOWER JUST OPENED;
(B) A FLOWER AT LATER STAGE.

31      Many recent observations go to show that mites, fungi and other fertilising agents can alter the shapes of flowers, and can cause petals to change into sepals, stamens into petals, and so on. Note also that flowers can be made double by mechanical irritation. It was this fact that first suggested that the alteration caused by the constant visits of bees, etc., may have altered, in many cases, the forms of flowers.

next point we notice is that in the salvia, as in the geranium, the anthers shed their pollen before the pistil is ripe. The pistil keeps out of the way till it is ripe, and then it bends over and strikes the back of the bee just where it caught the pollen from some younger salvia! By this beautiful plan, the salvia is often able to ripen its seeds by using the pollen of other flowers.

9. Plants that bear flowers of the pea-flower kind form a very large family among the irregular flowers; and so we shall pull to pieces the flower of this gorse-plant.

10. **A pea-flower—the gorse.** The two lower petals are joined to make a little boat, the keel. Look for the cargo of the boat, and you will find that it is ten stamens and a pistil. Often, too, it contains pollen that has been shaken off by the flower moving in the wind. Above the keel are two sails for the boat; and as the sails of a boat are its **wings**, we shall call these two petals the wings. Notice the two knobs in the wings that fit into hollows in the keel and so lock together wings and keel. Above them all is a broad petal that calls out to the bees: "Come hither," just as the standard of a great warrior called out to the people to gather under his flag. So we shall call this large petal the **standard**. Before the standard is hoisted, it serves as a kind

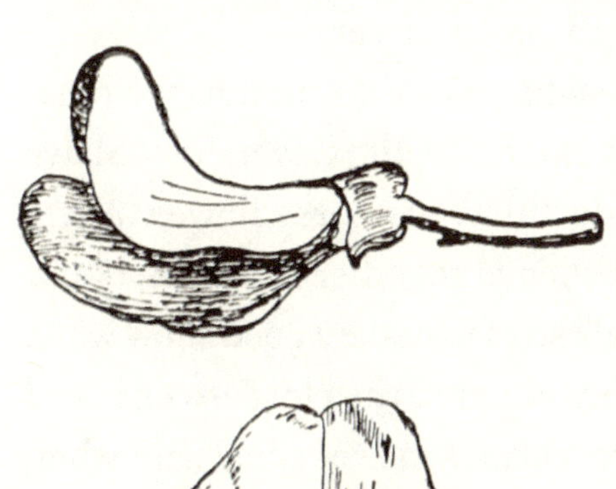


FIG 78
A Pea-flower; side view
and front view.

of roof to the keel. The pollen in the keel is thus protected from the rain.

11. **How the gorse-flower welcomes the bee.** Now, when the bee answers the call of the standard and buzzes up: "Here I am!" the flower is quite ready for her[32]. The bee alights on the wings, which are pressed down by her weight onto the keel. This causes the keel to unlock itself from the wings with a jerk, and the stamens to spring up suddenly out of the keel like Jack-in-the-box. As they rise, the pollen-dust explodes over the bee. Since the keel and the wings cannot lock themselves together again, a flower that has exploded looks quite different from one that is still locked. When no bee comes, the flower seems to be able to burst open of itself. This explosion may carry pollen to the pistil of the exploding blossom or to some other flower on the same bush. The explosion may be necessary also in order to let in air and light to help the pod to ripen[33].

12. **Another pea-flower—white clover.** And now we must stoop for a moment over this patch of white clover, for we have here a flower quite as wonderful as the gorse flower. Being very small, the flowers are bunched together in a cluster, and thrust upon a long flower-stalk so as to make a good show when the bees are wanted. When you smell the clover-scent, and remember that the bees have a keen sense of smell, and when you taste the delicious clover-honey, you will understand why the bees are so fond of the clover-flower. Look with your lens

32    The gorse is not a favourite of the bees who seem to visit it only when other flowers fail.

33    More observations seem to be needed as to the part that insects play in the fertilisation of this and other Leguminosae. In some flowers of this family the seed-cases seem to be self-fertilised before the flower becomes accessible to insects through the raising of the standard.

at one of the little flowers, and you will see that it is a complete pea-flower, with a very pretty calyx, and with the usual corolla, stamens, and pistil of the pea-flower.

13. **How the bee's time is saved.** The lower flowers in the clover bunch come out first, and then those higher up. When one of the lower flowers has been visited by a bee, it begins to gather itself round its seed-pod, and to throw itself back out of the way. Look at a clover cluster that has been in flower for a day or two, and you will see the little withered flowers that have been already visited by the bees. They are all hanging down out of the way, but the flowers that have not been visited stand straight up to catch the eye of the bee. When a bee comes up, it does not need to search to find out the flowers that have not been visited, and so no time is lost. This suits the bee, because it can get more honey, and it suits the clover because it can get more of its flowers visited. Can you wonder now that the clover-plant, with its beautiful leaves and its wonderfully-planned flowers, has spread all over the world? A great poet once lifted his hat to a fine rose; and, when you hear of a great man of science bending over a clover plant with wonder and delight, you will not now think it strange.

<u>Questions and Exercises:</u>

(1) Name all the flowers you know that are built on the pea-flower plan.

(2) Take a gorse flower to pieces, and find how the wings are locked at the base with the keel. Compare any of the native pea-flowers: sarsaparilla, native hop, native scarlet runner, birds' foot, trefoil, etc.

(3) How does the calyx of the gorse differ from that of the white clover?

(4) Take a gorse flower that is not yet exploded; press down gently with your finger on the wings and keel and watch what happens. Make experiments also with the lupine and the common lucerne (using pencil or straw).

(5) Take a "spent" flower-cluster of the white clover and find the ripening pods. Examine with lens. How are the pods protected while ripening?

(6) Note how in foxglove, salvia, and snapdragon the calyx is strengthened to support the door-step.

N.B. The grubs found when shelling pea-pods are due to eggs laid by flies in the ripening pod. Some pea-flowers have a plan for guarding against this.

**Composition Exercise:** Tell the story of a white clover cluster from the time the flower-stalk pushes it up to the time when the pods are ripe.

**Drawing Exercise**: Draw side by side a regular tubular flower and an irregular tubular flower.

XX.

# The Flower

<u>PART VI</u>

MORE ABOUT THE FLOWERS' DEBT TO INSECTS.

1. We have seen what the scarlet geranium owes to insects. Let us now see what other flowers owe to them.

2. **Honey-guides.** In our geranium you were delighted to find grooves leading to the honey-door. If you look at nasturtium, violet, gladiolus, and some of the Japanese lilies, you will be still more pleased. In these, and in many other flowers, the lines are like finger-posts bearing the words: "This way to the honey." And these guide-lines and spots and grooves make the flower more beautiful. How fine our roads and streets and houses and clothes will be when we too have learned to make all our useful things beautiful!

3. When looking for the guide-lines in the nasturtium, you noticed, I daresay, the hairs on the lower three petals. What are these?

4. **Hairs that act as fences to guard the honey.** Well, you must know that in England, the insect that helps the Indian cress to make its seed is the humble bee. The hairs do not hinder this great bee from reaching the honey, but they make a tangle which small honey thieves cannot get through. These hairs grow

on the part of the flower that bears the weight of the bee; and, indeed, the hairs may be caused by the bee pressing so often on this part. We know that hairs are very common in any part of a plant that is irritated in any way. In the ivy, it is only when the stem is touched by the wall that the hairs grow out that become air-roots. In the leaf-galls that are caused by little grubs irritating the leaves, there are often hairs inside and outside of the galls. This, then, would explain why the three lower petals are hairy, while the two upper petals have no hairs.

5. Sometimes, instead of a fence of hairs, a flower has a sticky patch that small insects cannot creep over. Here, again, the sticky fluid may be caused by the constant touch of the bee. This gives us a hint as to how honey-stores may have been formed to suit exactly the insect that visits the flower[34].

6. **The Honey-stores.** When the insects are small, or have short suckers, the honey is placed where it is easily reached. We saw this in the ivy flower, where the honey is on the shallow disc. Any fly can sip the ivy-honey. Where the insect has a long sucker, as in the humble bee, the honey is at the foot of a long tubular corolla or in a long spur below the flower. In each case, the length of the honey-tube fits exactly the length of the sucker of the insect friend. In the same way, the honey-pots of the

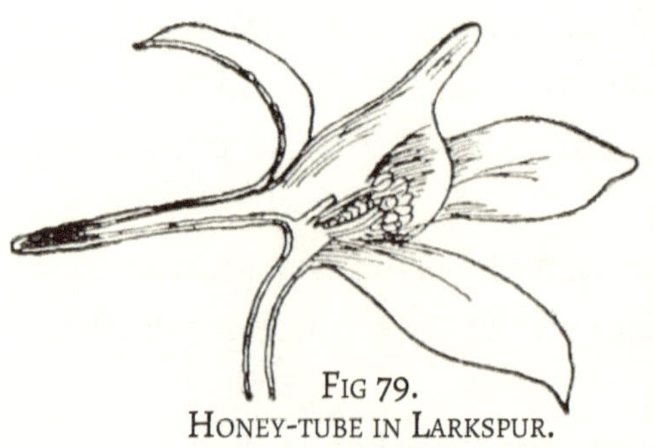

Fig 79.
Honey-tube in Larkspur.

---

34     Nectar is not confined to the flower, but may be found in other parts of some plants. In very good seasons there may even, in some plants, be an overflow of nectar in the leaves. At such times the leaves seem to make sugar too fast.

gum trees are fitted for the bills and tongues of the 'keets and other honey-eating birds. All this helps us to understand why we do not find honey in flowers that have never received the visits of insects.

7. And this sets us thinking too of the scent of flowers. I would not say that we owe all the scents of plants to the bees; for we have seen that perfume may help a plant in other ways. The scent of a plant is not always from the honey nor from the petals. You know how pleasant is the scent of sweet-briar leaves and gum leaves; and even the wood of some trees has a pleasant smell. But probably we owe many of the delightful scents of the garden to the visits of insects. If you look at those flowers that use the wind to scatter their pollen, you will find that they have no scent.

8. **The charm and the mystery of scent.** When we have said all that we can to account for the perfume of the plant, there is still much that we cannot explain. The scent of a plant is in some ways more real to us than the plant itself. Here and there in Europe, the travelling Australian can see a gum tree that recalls his fatherland, but nothing that the eye can see can take him back to his boyhood like a whiff of wattle scent from a London or Paris flower shop[35]. Little wonder that this invisible mysterious something that we call scent is often called the soul of the plant. How close the tie is between scent and plant is shown by a very wonderful fact. When caught and bottled, the perfume of a flower shows a strange excitement when the time of the flowering of the plant comes round. The scent becomes troubled

35    A few gum trees from Australia are to be found here and there on the coast of the Mediterranean; and our silver wattle is now grown in the Riviera.

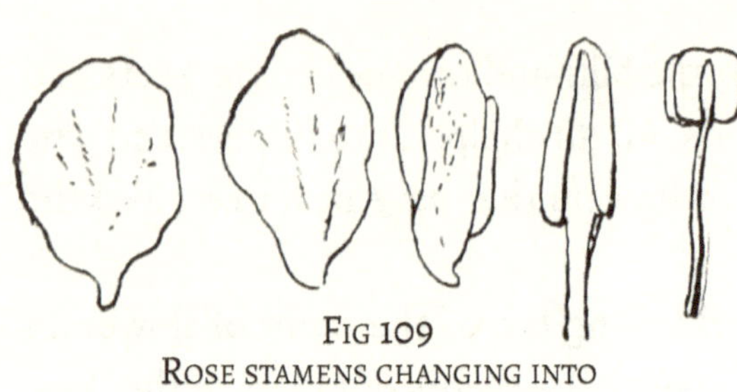

Fig 109

Rose stamens changing into petals as we pass from the centre of the rose outwards.

and the fragrance stronger!

9. And now we must look carefully at the colour of flowers, for this is the greatest debt that man owes to the bees and butterflies and other insects that visit flowers.

10. **The colour of flowers**. In our scarlet geranium we found that the large gay petals were due to the visits of insects. We know from the fossil flowers found in rocks that in far-past times, when there were no insects, there were no petals. How, then, were the petals made? Pull off the petal of a **monthly rose**, one by one. As you come near to the centre you will often find a petal that is half petal and half stamen, and when quite close to the centre, you may find a stamen that is just beginning to be a petal. You can often find the same thing in many other flowers that have become double in the garden. We know, too, how single flowers can be made double by the gardener, and how he can make the petals larger and richer in colour. We guess from all this that the visits of insects have caused stamens to broaden into petals, and petals to become gay in colour. When a double flower is neglected, the petals often change again into stamens. Indeed, if you sow the seed from a garden rose, you will often get a rosebush bearing single flowers like the hedge rose. Now, since yellow is the colour of pollen and of many stamens, we are not surprised to find that many of the simplest and oldest flowers are yellow. If you take a walk in the fields on a spring

day and watch the colours of the flowers, I think that you will find that yellow is more common than any other colour.

11. Pink seems to be the next most common colour, and then come the rarer purples and blues[36]. Many of the highest flowers—the flowers that have been shaped specially for the bees—are blue. Simple, regular flowers, like the poppy or the buttercup, are rarely blue. The rose is a simple regular flower, as you may see by looking at a hedge rose. Can you find a blue rose? The portulaca is a simple regular flower; can you find a blue one? Almost any flower may have a white variety. You will notice, too, that when a flower, like chickweed, learns to make seed without insect help, it often becomes white or pale-coloured.

12. **How the bees paint flowers.** Have you ever noticed that some insects, in seeking honey, fly or creep from one flower to another; but that bees do not mix different kinds of honey in this way? That is one reason why the higher flowers give no welcome to the lower kind of insects. It does no good to the dandelion if a fly comes to it laden with the pollen of the thistle. Watch the bees at work in a field where the yellow flatweed is in flower, and you will see that they keep to this flower. Where there are beds of the same kind of flower, as phlox or portulaca, it would be interesting to know if the bee visits one colour more than another. Does the bee visit a white portulaca as readily as a pink one?[37] One thing is certain: the bees mix the colours by taking pollen from one to another. If you have a bed of phlox

36      Of 27 flowers collected on Mt. Kosciusko by Mr. Maiden, of Sydney, 19 were yellow, 7 pink, and only 1 was blue.

37      In preferring one kind of flower to another, the bee is but little influenced by colour. It is influenced mainly by the amount and accessibility of the honey or pollen. This is why a bee will often neglect the finest garden flowers for gum tree flowers or small greenish flowers that do not catch the eye at all.

of six different colours, it is quite likely that next year you will have seven or eight varieties from the seed taken from the six kinds. Try it. A boy who prides himself on his beautiful phlox beds tells me that he counted 40 different kinds last summer. Now, all these varieties have sprung from one or two kinds that were got wild in Texas; and we owe the variety to the visiting insects.

13. We have still much to learn about the colours of flowers and about the way in which flowers and insects work together; but of one thing we are sure: the flowers that have been most visited by insects have become more and more beautiful, and more and more interesting to man[38]. Take away from the flowers the form, the colour, the scent that they owe to the insects, and how much of the wonder and beauty of the world would be lost! It is quite possible that, as hive bees become more plentiful in Australia, some of our wild flowers may become larger and gayer than they are to-day.

<u>Questions and Exercises:</u>

(1)   Why are most of the flowers that invite night-flying moths white or yellow? Why are they generally heavily scented?

(2)   Look for the honey-guide lines in ivy-pelargonium, gladiolus, nasturtium, and in many other flowers.

(3)   It is said that Australian flowers have no scent. Can you name any of our flowering plants that are fragrant in leaf or bloom? Any shrubs or trees?

(4)   Bite the honey-spur of the nasturtium. Name any other flowers with honey-spurs.

(5)   Count the kinds of plants with yellow flowers that you meet

38     It is when in contact with higher *life*—the life of the insect and the life of man—that plant life shows its greatest beauty. We have here a most suggestive thought.

in a spring walk. Compare with flowers of other colours. Note the colour of the plants that are most abundant.

(6)   Some plants, like the sorrel-weed (sour-grass), cause patches of colour that can be seen and recognised a long way off. Name any other plants in your district that cause colour-patches of this kind.

(7)   The red and yellow tints on some young gum trees are as beautiful as coloured flowers. Tell of any other leaves whose colours you have admired.

**Composition Exercise:** Try to imagine what a garden would be like if insects had never visited flowers. Describe it.

**Drawing Exercise:** Draw any flower that has a special honey-tube.

XXI.

# The Flower

<u>PART VII.</u>

WIND-FERTILIZED FLOWERS.

1. **Flowers that use the wind to scatter their pollen**. Flowers cannot leave the place where they were born; and so, in order to scatter their pollen, they must make use of carriers. We have seen how some of them pay the insects to do this work; and now we have to look at those flowers that make use of the wind. This is a common plan among the trees and grasses. We shall look first of all at the oak, which is one of the many trees that use this way of spreading their pollen.

2. **How the oak tree makes seed.** Look at an oak tree in the springtime, just as the beautiful light green leaves are breaking out of the buds; and you will see long, loose tassels or catkins that wave in the breeze. Use your lens, and you will see that the tassel is made up of clusters of small flowers that bear pollen. Shake the tassel, and a shower of pollen will fall. There are no pistils in these tassel-flowers of the oak; so that we guess at once that the pistil-bearing flowers are either on other parts of the tree or on other oak trees. Ah! Here they are; on the same branch a little higher up, and snugly sheltered between the leaf-stalk and the stem. These pistil-bearing flowers are so small that you

might easily miss them! So small is the flower that makes the acorn that makes the oak!

3. Many trees that make seed on this plan have the pollen-bearing flowers on one tree, and the pistil-bearing flowers on a separate tree. Of this kind are the poplars.

4. In most trees that use the wind as a pollen-carrier, the pollen is made and scattered before the leaves come out. You may see this very clearly in the elm tree. The flowers open, and ripen, and fall before the leaves appear. The spring wind blows them about the street while the branches overhead are still bare. In this

FIG 83
CATKIN OF OAK.

way, pollen is not caught by the leaves, which have no need of it, and is more likely to fall on the pistil flowers that do need it. Sometimes the wind is not blowing in the right direction, and so the pollen falls where it can do no good; but the tree makes so much pollen that some of the dust is almost sure to fall where it is wanted. Strike the pollen-flowers of a Scotch fir-tree, or of any of the pines, and see what a shower of pollen comes out! Sometimes, indeed, there is so much pollen in the air when the trees and grasses are making their seed that people become ill through breathing it. They get what is called hay-fever, and are sometimes ordered to the seaside where there is little pollen in the air. In countries where pines abound, the rains of spring are sometimes coloured yellow, and the ignorant people talk of sulphur-showers!

5. **How the common plantain makes seed.** And now, if you look for the common plantain, sometimes called rib-grass, we

shall examine a plant that uses the wind to bear its pollen. This plant lifts up its spike of brown tiny flowers on a long tough stalk. Very likely you have played at the game of striking the heads of the rib-grass one against the other till one of the stalks breaks.

6. Each little flower on the spike has a tiny calyx, a chaffy corolla, and stamens, and pistil. The stigma is hairy in order to catch the pollen easily as it floats past in the air; and the long stamens hang out freely, so that the pollen may be readily blown off by the wind. Notice carefully that nearly all the grasses have stamens and stigmas of this kind (figs. 85 and 86). Like the cloverhead, the flowers of the plantain ripen from the base of the spike upwards; and, if you watch some particular spike from day to day, you will see how the circle of white broad anthers slowly moves up the brown spike, till perhaps only a solitary stamen on the very top waves its white anthers in the air. No insect visits these flowers; and the sole purpose of the long tough stalks is to catch the wind.

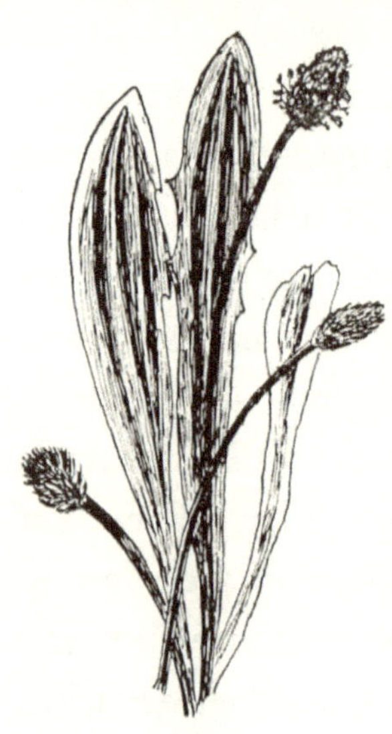

Fig 84
Plantain (rib-grass).

7. **The flower of the wheat plant.** And now we shall go back to the wheat-field, and watch again the heads bending to the breeze. This time we shall look more closely at the wheat-flower. First of all, we take notice that each flower hangs in such a way that it moves at the slightest breath of the wind. The whole wheat-plant also bends easily to the wind, and the pollen on its slender stalks is so light and loose that it readily floats into

Fig 85
FLOWER OF WHEAT,
WITH SCALES
REMOVED, SHOWING
LOOSE ANTHERS AND
FEATHERY PISTIL.

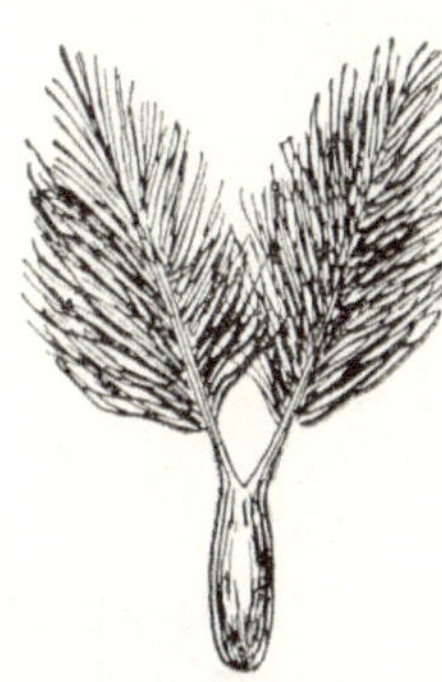

Fig 86
PISTIL OF A GRASS,
SHOWING THE
FEATHERY STIGMA.

the air. On removing the chaffy scales, we find three stamens, and a pistil with two feathery stigmas. With its long swaying stamens, loose pollen, and feathery stigmas, the plant has no difficulty in setting its seed.

8. It is the wind that bears to the green wheat-blade the food that builds it up, food that no eye can see. By the wind's help, too, the wheat-plant makes its seed. And thus, by help of something that we cannot see, is made the grain that furnishes man's table with food. Here, again, we find that the things that we cannot see are often more important than the things that we can look at and handle.

In the maize plant, the pollen-bearing flowers form the tallest part of the plant. The pistil-bearing flowers, with the silken tassel, are lower down, and at first are almost hidden by the leaves.

<u>Questions and Exercises:</u>

(1)   Why are very small flowers generally green?

(2)   The plan of using the wind as pollen-carrier is more common among trees and tall grasses than among other plants. How is this?

(3)   Why is honey generally absent from the flowers that use the wind to carry the pollen?

(4)   The common dock makes its seed by help of the wind. Examine the flowers.

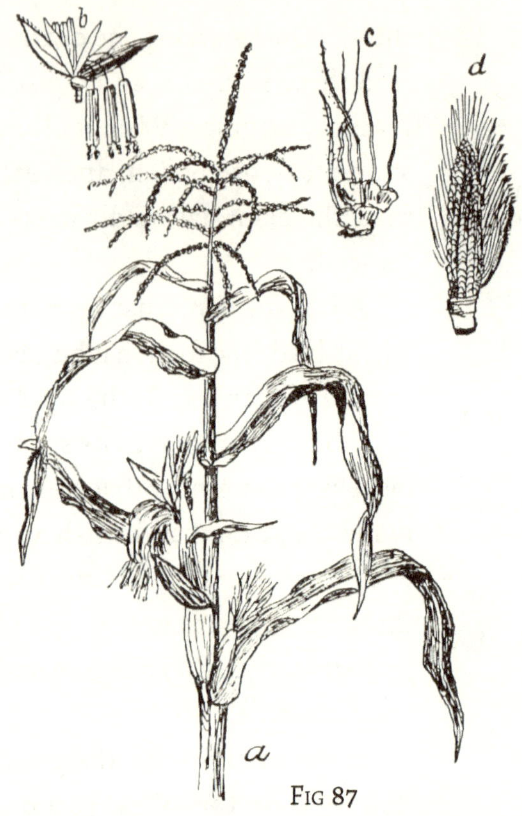

Fɪɢ 87

(*a*) Maize plant showing the pollen-bearing flowers (tassels). (*b*) The same plant showing the seed-bearing flowers magnified. (*c*) Pistils, showing the growing grains. (*d*) Head or cob.

(5)　Stand below a willow tree in the time of flower, and try to find out its plan of making seed. Is it wind-fertilized?

(6)　Examine the flower of native couch grass. Look for the stamens with their white loose anthers, and for the white or pink pistil. Use lens.

**Composition Exercise:** Describe the flowers of any tree or grass that uses the wind as pollen-carrier.

**Drawing Exercise:** Make a drawing of a branch (of any tree) bearing catkins.

XXII.

# Fruits and Seeds

<u>PART I.</u>

HOW SEEDS ARE SPREAD.

1. When young birds are old enough to seek their own food, the old birds drive them away from their "selection." If they remained where they were born, there would not be food enough for all.

2. Why do plants send their seeds out into the world? In the same way, a plant has its own bit of ground, and it needs it all in order to live and thrive. Thousands of seeds never become plants, because they cannot get root-room and leaf-room. A Cape-weed that spreads its broad rosette over the earth may smother a hundred little plants, and so with every flat weed that succeeds in life. Indeed, very few of the seeds of wild flowers ever become plants. Some seeds fall on stony ground where they cannot get a start; others are eaten by birds, or beasts, or insects. Even when they do get a start in life, they seldom become full-grown. Some are choked, as we have seen, by other plants; others are eaten or crushed, and others die of thirst. You see, then, why plants are fitted with a hundred plans for spreading their seeds far and wide. How well this is done you may judge by an example of great interest.

145

3. **How a vacant island was stocked with plants.** Some years ago there was an island called Krakatoa, a few days' sail north of Australia. A great volcanic eruption destroyed this island, so that no living thing was left upon it. To-day there are many different kinds of plants, none of which was taken to the island by man. How did they get there? Some of them from seeds carried by the waves; others from seeds borne by the wind, and the rest from seeds left by passing birds. Well, we shall look at all those ways and at others besides. When we examined the scarlet geranium, we found that the seeds were slung away from the parent-plant; and we shall look first of all at this plan for spreading seed.

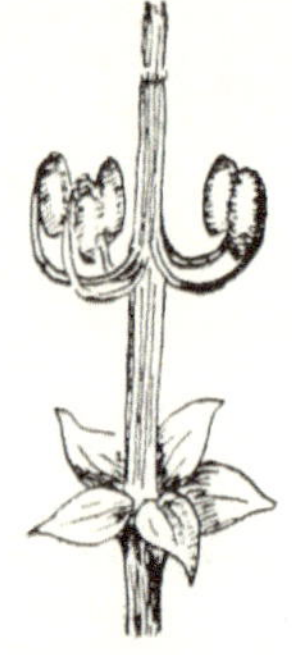

Fig 94
Ripe fruit of
a Geranium.

4. **Seeds that are jerked out of the fruit.** All the different kinds of geraniums—garden and wild—have this way of spreading their seed. When you see a plant bearing a seed-case that looks like a stork's bill, long and pointed, you may be sure that it is a member of this family. If the seed-case be quite ripe, you may find that it requires only a touch to make it fire off the seed. In a wild state, the plant often gets this touch from a passing animal, and there is a good chance that the seed will catch on the fur and get a free ride.

5. But all the plants that use this plan do not sling out the seed like the geranium. Look for a ripe pod of the little field-sorrel, with the

Fig 95
Ripening seed-cases
of a Stork's bill.

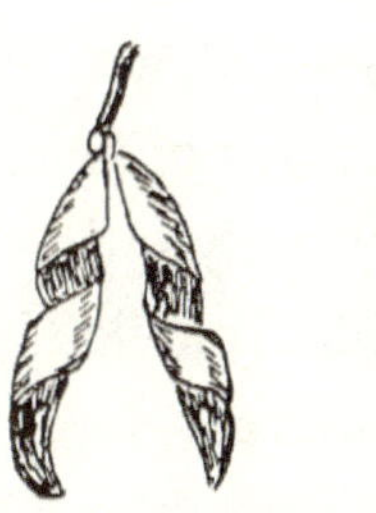

FIG 96

PEA FLOWER POD, JERKING OUT ITS SEED.

yellow flowers. You will find plenty of them in late spring and in autumn in most fields. When the pod is ripe, it fires out the seed by suddenly twisting up the pod, just as you can shoot an orange-seed across a room by pressing it between finger and thumb. When you are looking at ripe sorrel-pods on a hot day with face close to the ground, you may get a volley of the seed against your cheek. If you place a few ripe seed-pods upon a long table, you may be able to measure how far the seed is thrown.

6. When you walk among gorsebushes on a hot-wind day, you may hear the pods going *pop, pop,* on every side; and if you hold up a newspaper and touch one or two ripe pods, you will see with what force the tiny peas are thrown against the paper.

One of the commonest of our climbing plants for covering fences is the dolichos. You will know it by its compound leaf with three leaflets, and its pink pea-flower. The ripe pod, in hot weather, suddenly curls up, and throws the little dark pea from three to ten feet.

7. **Water-borne seeds.** Then there are the seeds that are borne away from the parent-plant by water. After violent rain and wind, you may often find in a field that is half-bare of grass, ridges of dry leaves and seeds that have been washed along the ground for some distance. Every flood, too, in our rivers carries down seeds, which lodge on banks or on neighbouring flats. If a few wattle-trees were planted near the source of a river, they

would soon in this way begin to scatter wattle-trees all down the course of the river. It is to this that we owe the groves of silver wattle that make our river-courses so beautiful in early spring.

8. If you look at the rubbish that has been caught from flood-waters by bushes or rushes, you will often find fruits and seeds. It may be long before these get covered by moist earth; but many of our native fruits are very hard, and these can wait for years for a chance to grow.

9. **Sea-borne seeds.** As to seeds that are borne by the sea, I shall speak only of a fruit which you know well—the coco-nut.

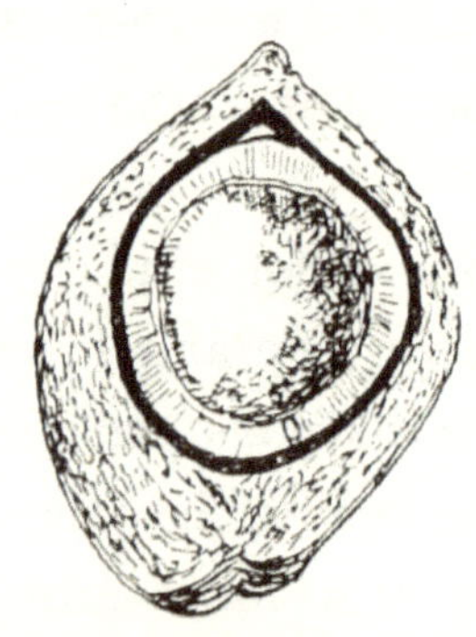

Fig 97

Coco-nut showing the husk, the hard shell and the white flesh.

You know the hard nut and you have eaten the white flesh; but not everyone has seen the thick outer husk. This husk, which in many countries is used for scrubbing floors, is light and strong. When the nut drops from the palm tree into the sea, the husk enables it to float, and it is often borne to distant islands. When a new island is raised to the surface by coral-insects, the coco-palm is often the first plant to grow.

10. **Pond weeds and seaweeds.** Many pond plants throw off little green buds which float about till they find a good place to strike root and become new plants! Still more wonderful are certain seaweeds. These sea plants throw off buds or seeds that swim about with the help of waving hairs. After wandering for a time, they moor themselves to a rock, and settle down for life.

11. **How a grass-seed may sow itself.** On the ripe seed of sweet vernal grass and some other grasses, there is a bristle or awn.

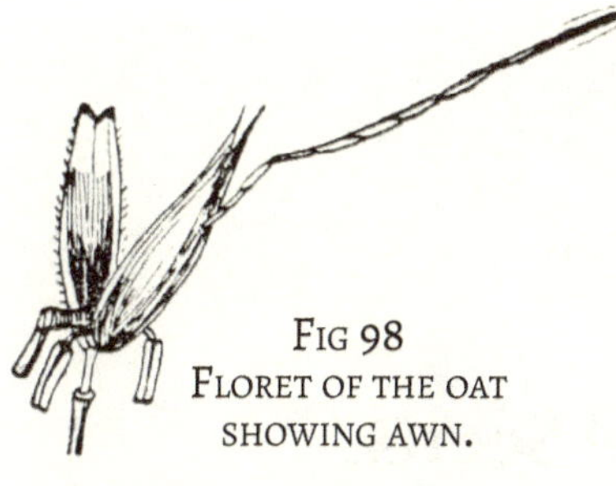

Fig 98
Floret of the oat
showing awn.

Sometimes this bristle is rough enough to catch on to animals, but its main use is to bury the seed in the ground! The plan is quite simple. When dry, the awn coils up; but when damp from dew or rain, it straightens itself out again. Every time this change takes place, the seed crawls and wriggles, and is sometimes in this way pushed into sand or into a crack where the rains may cover it with soil.

<u>Questions and Exercises:</u>

(1)   Name any plants that spread in rosettes smothering smaller plants.

(2)   Take ripe seed of gorse or dolichos or balsam indoors, and try to measure how far the seed is thrown. Why is the garden-balsam called *Touch-me-not*?

(3)   Compare the following pods that jerk seed: Gorse, field-sorrel, dolichos, common broom.

(4)   Dock-weed seed are borne down a river. A single seed of the dock sinks when put into water; (try it). Explain Nature's plan for making it float.

(5)   Can you find any other plants that live on river-flats that have "floats" of any kind for their seed?

**Composition Exercise:** Write the story of a silver wattle pod that travelled down a river and made a new tree.

**Drawing Exercise:** Draw a dolichos pod (*a*) before it has thrown its seed; (*b*) after it has thrown its seed.

XXIII.

# Fruits and Seeds

PART II.

HOW SEEDS ARE SPREAD BY ANIMALS.

1. And now we have to see how seeds are spread by animals.

2. **How juicy, coloured fruits are spread.** Just as flowers put forth gay petals to draw the bees, so many fruits become sweet and coloured to draw the birds or other animals. We have seen that many plants have insect friends that come to their flowers. In the same way, many plants have bird or animal friends that come when the seeds are ripe. It is to let these friends know when the seed is ripe that the fruit becomes red or yellow, black or white. And it is to pay them for carrying away the seeds that the fruits are juicy and sweet. In Australia it is not easy to understand all about these friendships between plant and bird and beast, because most of our fruit-trees are from abroad.

3. Some of our native birds have learned to eat the fruits of trees that have been brought into Australia. The little silver-eye is just as fond of mulberries as of any native fruit; and the 'keets often come to the orchard in swarms when the plums are ripe. The prickly-pear is not a native plant, but our birds have become fond of its yellow fruit, and have scattered the seed so that the plant has overrun and spoiled many rich pieces of land.

4. **Colours of fruits and flowers compared.** Have you ever noticed that fruits often have colours that you rarely find among the flowers? Purple is a common colour among wild berries, but rare among wild flowers. Black is rarely found as a flower-colour, but is common among berries. The birds that eat the berries seem to have different tastes in colour from the bees that visit the flowers. Perhaps another reason is that a good contrast is needed between the berries and the leaves. If the berry of Virginia creeper were red instead of dark-coloured, it could not be seen against the red autumn leaves. And now we pass to the seeds that are neither juicy nor coloured but that are produced in great number.

5. **How small dry seeds are spread by birds.** Perhaps you have never noticed the small hard seeds that fall from ripe grasses and weeds. It is not easy to see them among thick grass, but now and then, on a bare bit of ground, you can see the seeds lying in hundreds. You must look for these, for seeds often have the colour of the ground they fall on. You know how every bare patch in a field breaks into green after the rains of autumn. This growth is from the seeds that have escaped the birds.

6. A large weed often grows many thousands of seeds. It is said that a single plant of common purslane—the thick, reddish-green weed that overruns the garden-beds in summer—can produce 1,250,000 seeds in one season! If every seed from one plant grew into a plant, the whole world would soon be overrun with this wonderful weed.[39] You see now what keeps the birds busy in a field from morning to night!

---

39     The First Australians used to get fat on this seed. They would collect great heaps of the weed and then shake out the seeds.

7. Many of these small hard seeds are destroyed in the stomachs of the birds, but some pass through the birds unhurt. Also, you must remember that many birds expel seeds from their mouths in pellets. These seeds are not hurt, and, indeed, such seeds germinate more easily than ordinary seeds. Crows often eject pellets of seed, and probably do more to spread plants than any other birds.

8. **Sticky seeds.** Some of the small dry seeds, such as the seeds of rib-grass and groundsel (fig. 99), become sticky; and this helps them to catch on to birds and animals. Among shrubs, too, we have some plants like Victorian laurel that have smooth seed-cases enclosing sticky seeds. Others, like the plumbago, have a sticky calyx that closes over the ripe seed. You know the plumbago with its pale blue flowers that give beauty to many an ugly fence? After the long, blue tube-corolla

Fig 99
Groundsel.

has done its work, it twists up so as to form a kind of hook. Meantime, the calyx that encloses the fruit frees itself from the stem and hangs out to catch on to animals by its sticky hooks. Though quite detached from its stalk, the fruit holds on to the plant by these hooks, or by the withered, twisted corolla. Brush against the plant when the seeds are ripe, and notice how the seed-cases stick to your coat.

FIG 100
BURR-MEDICK (YELLOW CLOVER).
THE SEED-CASES ARE SPIRALLY
TWISTED INTO A PRICKLY BALL.

9. **Hooked seeds.** Many seeds, again, cling to animals by the help of hooks. The best known are the common sheep's burr and the Bathurst burr, but there are many others that do not stick so well as these. Such seed-cases cannot fly, nor can they jerk out their seed; but they lie in wait for a carrier. A horse lies down to roll. What a chance to stick a seed on his coat! A sheep passes on its way to grass 100 miles off. Here is a chance to travel! A boy picks a burr to play at burr-throwing. What a chance to get away to fresh fields! The mischief done by these burr plants is enormous. When the cockle-burr was first noticed in Queensland, £50 might have cleared it all out of Australia. Since that time it has cost Australia many thousands of pounds, and no one knows what it will cost in the end. I might give a whole chapter to telling you of the damage done by the Bathurst burr, and how it has spread from land to land. In 1835, a shipload of horses was brought from Chili to Australia. In the tails and manes of the horses were seeds of the burr, which we now call the Bathurst burr because it was first noticed at Bathurst. It is said that five minutes' work would have killed the first few plants that appeared. This would have saved to Australia

BRANCH AND FRUIT OF THE BATHURST BURR: A MUCH-BRANCHED SHRUB 1 TO 3FT. HIGH WITH MANY 3 PRONGED SPINES: FRUIT EGG SHAPED WITH HOOKED PRICKLES.

millions of pounds sterling. Examine the plant for yourselves. Look at its wonderful seeds with your lens. Watch the plant for a whole year till you know its ways, and then you will understand why it is such a terrible and dangerous pest.

10. **How birds may carry seeds.** You have often watched a duck with its tail in the air and its bill in the mud at the bottom of a pond. Now, among the things that it finds in the mud are seeds. Pond-mud is often full of seeds, and when a water-fowl that has been wading in a pond flies away, it often carries seeds in the mud on its legs. Eighty-two different kinds of plants were grown from seeds taken from the legs of a partridge. Birds often fly great distances, and now and then are blown far away by great gales of wind. In this way, as well as by seed-balloons, seeds may travel on the wings of the wind.

11. **How seeds are spread by man.** There stand in Rome to-day the ruins of the Coliseum, a great circus of stone. Among these ruins, rare plants are found, due, it is supposed, to the seeds brought from the ends of the earth on the sandals of Roman soldiers. In similar ways, the Crusaders brought new

Fig 101
Common sorrel-weed.

plants to England. For many centuries, ships have carried fodder for cattle and grain for fowls, and in this way seeds have often been swept from the deck to the sea and borne to land. The cockle-burr is said to have sprung up in New Zealand from ballast landed by a ship from South America. Seeds, again, are often contained in the straw or grass used to pack cases of goods. To this we owe many of our weeds. Then there is the trade in seed from one country to another. When you sow clover-seed bought in Europe, you may sow with it weed-seeds that are so like the clover-seed that they are not noticed. We have in Australia the hog-weed, sorrel-weed (fig. 101), sow-thistle, the scarlet pimpernel, lucerne-dodder, and many other weeds and wild flowers of Europe. The cockle-burr is said to have been brought into Australia with cotton seed sown in Queensland.

12. Plants in pots and "cuttings" are brought to Australia from all parts of the world. In the Melbourne Botanic Gardens, you may see a great weeping-willow that was grown from a "cutting" taken from the tree that grows over the grave of Napoleon at St. Helena. And so it has come to pass that our gardens are made beautiful by the finest trees and flowers of many countries. God did not mean the rose of Persia to be kept in one land only; and

so the rose of Persia is to-day in many lands. So is it with all that is good in flower and fruit.

## Questions and Exercises:

(1) Give the colours of all the berries you have noticed. What colours are the most common?

(2) Can you name any birds that eat (a) the pink berries of the pepper-tree, (b) the red berries of the Cape thorn hedge?

(3) Look with lens at the calyx of the plumbago flower at various stages of ripeness, and tell what you see.

(4) Find the large, tall summer weed with strong branching red stems and reddish-green tiny flowers. Shake a ripe spike over white paper, and look at the many little seeds, shiny and black like the body of a garden ant.

(5) Find a ripe spike of the broad-leaved plantain. Count the seeds in one of the little egg-shaped pods. Count the pods on the spike, and the spikes on the plant, and reckon up the total number of seeds.

(6) Over a million seeds may be produced by one large weed. What becomes of them?

(7) Some seeds resemble insects, and may possibly be carried off by insect-eating birds. Examine the seed of the castor-oil plant, (a) with the sheath on, (b) when stripped of its sheath.

(8) In what way do the seeds of the following plants travel: burr-medick (yellow clover), forget-me-not, pittosporum (Victorian laurel), carrot?

(9) No roads in Australia have so many weeds as the travelling stock routes. Explain.

**Composition Exercise:** A Bathurst burr in a field near Melbourne sprang from seed grown on a Darling River station. Tell the story of the travels of the burr.

**Drawing Exercise:**

Draw and colour a bunch of berries or of any coloured fruit.

Draw (*a*) a burr of the Bathurst burr plant, (*b*) a single hook of the burr (enlarged).

XXIV.

# Fruits and Seeds

PART III.

HOW SEEDS ARE CARRIED BY THE WIND.

1. We saw how some seeds manage to travel by hooking themselves to animals. But this, of course, is possible only in the case of plants that are near to the ground. When the plants are over seven or eight feet high, the seeds cannot be brushed off by animals. And this is why many trees depend on the wind to carry off their seeds.

2. **Tumble-weeds.** Even in the case of low plants, the wind is sometimes used to scatter seed. The branches of some low plants and grasses become brittle when the seeds are ripe, and are broken off and carried away by the first high wind. Some plants, indeed, break off close to the root, and are blown away entire. On many of the wide open plains of Australia, there is a tumble-weed of this kind. It is often a good-sized shrub, growing as high as a small boy. This shrub grows into a large, round ball; big enough to be a giant's football; and the wind plays with it over the plains, this way and that, for miles at a time, until, one day, it sticks on a bush or fence. Even a fence does not always stop these plant-balls. One is piled up on another, just as boys give each other "a back up" in climbing a wall, and then

157

a plant-ball comes rolling up before a brisk wind and clears the fence! At Mildura, the boys call a plant of this kind the "roly-poly." Well, you can see how a tumble-weed like this sows its seeds as it rolls over the plain.

3. **How the poppy scatters seed.** Did you ever notice how a poppy plant makes full use of its height in getting its seed scattered? Round the root of the pretty seed-box is a kind of eave, and under the shelter of this eave you will find the holes by which the seeds escape. Strike a ripe seed-pod, and you may see some seeds fall out easily, but others can be jerked out only by a high wind that throws them to some distance. You see now why the poppy head stands straight up as high as it can reach, and why it has so stiff a stem.

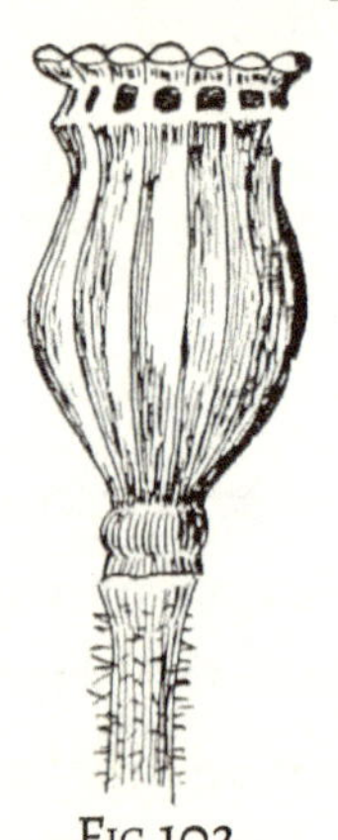

Fig 102
Poppy head, showing the holes by which the seeds escape.

4. **A balloon of silky hairs.** Another plan for scattering seed, much used by ground plants, is a balloon of silky hairs. Nearly all the flowers built on the plan of the dandelion have a balloon of some kind; but the most familiar plant to us is the flatweed. The yellow flower on the long stalk of the flatweed gives more colour to our fields in winter than any other flower. The balloon of the flatweed is a beautiful object when seen through a lens, but it is not so perfect as that of the dandelion. If you can get a dandelion that has just hoisted its balloon to the wind, try in how many puffs you can blow away all the seeds. In some lands the children say as they blow: "One o'clock, two o'clock," and so on. Well, we shall suppose that you have puffed them all away except one, that stands alone on

FIG 103
HEAD OF DANDELION, WITH
SEED READY FOR FLIGHT.

the pitted disc. I shall ask you to draw this seed with its balloon. You cannot draw the beautiful silky sheen of the hairs, but your drawing may show how wonderfully the seed is planned for travel. All the thistles use this plan for making their seeds travel. Can you wonder that thistles soon spread over a whole country?

5. **How the willow-herb scatters its seed.** In few plants is the balloon of hairs so delicate as in the willow-herb—a plant often found on river flats and other damp places. It is a plant from two to four feet high, bearing a pink flower, that ripens into a long, slender pod. When this pod splits, it shows many small seeds, each of which has a delicate tuft of silky hairs. The pod opens from the top downwards, and, as the topmost balloons are blown away, the lower ones push the pod farther apart so that the wind may blow them away in their turn. Look at these beautiful seeds with your lens, and you may find that some of the seeds are not fully grown, but these help with their balloons to float away the heavier ripe seeds. But, indeed, none of the

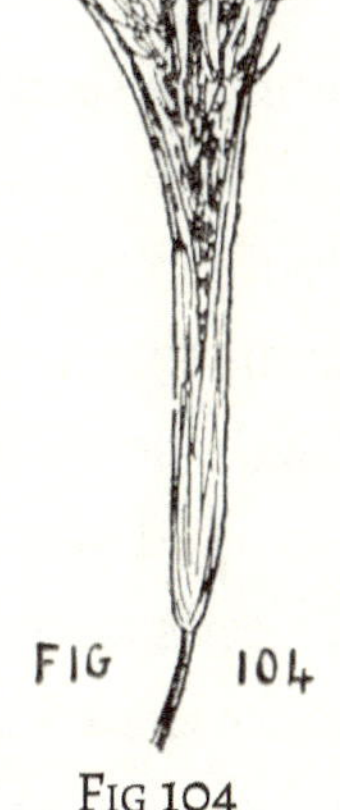
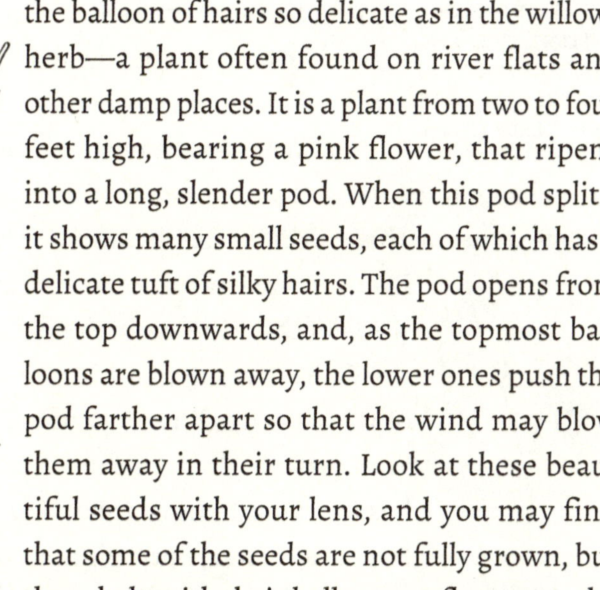


FIG 104
SEED CASE OF
WILLOW-HERB,
SPLITTING OPEN
TO LET THE SEED
FLY AWAY.

seed is heavy; for it would take about 30,000 of them to weigh as much as one broad bean!

6. **Trees that have hairy seeds.** Among the trees, too, some make use of the balloon of hairs. Look at ripe seeds of the plane tree, or of the willow, or of the oleander, and you will see the hairy seeds ready for a flight. Have you noticed how tough the fruit-stalks of the plane tree are, and how tightly they hold on (FIG 105) to the tree? Break up one of the fruit balls, and you will find that the seeds are feathered for flight. Now, if the ball fell easily to the ground, the seeds would have little chance of flying. Hence, the balls hang on tightly, often through the whole winter, swinging and banging against the wood in every gale, till the seeds are loosened and fly away.

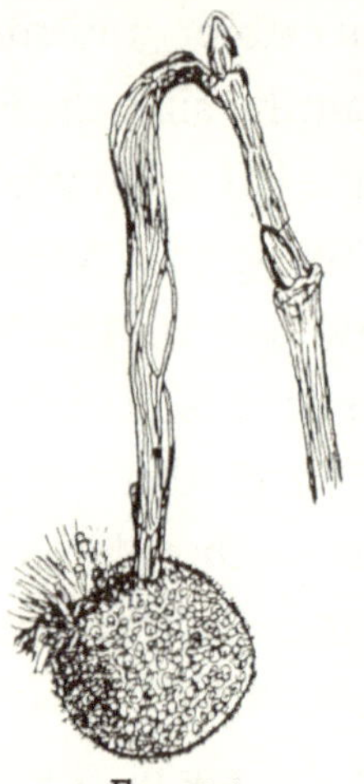

Fig 105

Fruit ball of plane tree. The ball is planning to break up to let the seeds escape.

7. **Trees that have flat or winged seeds.** But the plan most in use among the trees that use the wind as a seed-carrier is that of the flat, light seeds or winged seeds.

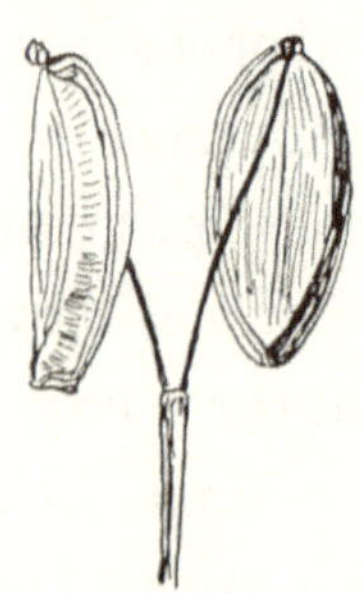

Fig 106

Flat-winged seeds of parsnip.

Even among low plants we find some that have seeds of this kind, as in the flat, light seeds of the Cape love-lily, and in the winged seeds of the parsnip. But most of the seeds of this kind grow high up in the air where the wind has a chance to blow them to a distance. The hop is not a tree, but it climbs on trees or high poles, and so we are not surprised to find that its seeds are winged. One of the simplest of

Fig 107
Winged seed
of pine.

winged seeds is that of the pine. If you break open the hard scales of a pine cone[40], you will see that each seed has a wing.

8. Notice carefully that in many pines the wing is not evenly balanced. Can you guess the purpose of this? The longer the seed takes to reach the ground, the more chance the wind has of blowing it away. Now, if two winged seeds fall from the same point at the same moment, one of which is well-balanced and the other not, which seed will take the longer to reach the ground? Some trees, however, have winged seed with the wings almost evenly balanced. You will see this in the elm, and in the plane tree that is called the sycamore. But the slightest unevenness in the balance serves the purpose.

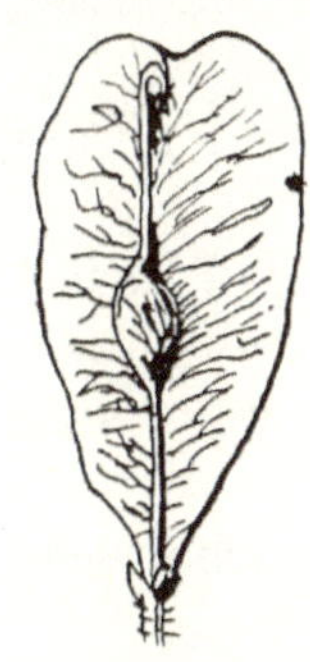

Fig 108
Winged seed
of elm.

9. Even without wings, a cluster of seed-cases blown off a high tree in a storm can travel some distance. Look at the ground near a tall gum tree after a storm, and you may see how gum tree seed-cases are sometimes scattered. The seeds of gum trees, however, often escape from the seed-cases while these are still on the tree. The seeds are, as a rule, small and light, and when they escape from seed-cases on a high branch, they may be carried a good way by the wind.

10. Of the wonders of seed travel I have not told you one half; but I can tell you of only one more.

11. **Seeds that cannot be seen.** Some of the seeds we have

40      A hatchet may be needed if the pine cone be young. Cones often hang for years before the seeds fall out. Alternate sun and rain cause the scales to open, and in this way the seeds become at last free.

been looking at are very small, but they can all be seen with the naked eye. Now, there are millions of seeds so small that they can float in the air, and can be seen only with the help of a microscope. It is these unseen seeds that coat an old apple tree with lichen, and a damp rock with moss. God has so made the world that no part of it can long remain bare or ugly; and so, on the places where large plants could not live, minute plants spring into life. Even an old fence rail is often beautiful.

<u>Questions and Exercises:</u>

(1) How does the native blue-bell scatter its seed?

(2) Break open a ripe seed-ball of the plane tree and find out its secret of seed-dispersal.

(3) Which is the prettiest seed balloon you know? Make a list of some of the finest.

(4) Collect a number of different kinds of flat or winged seeds.

(5) Give the colours of the lichens of your district.

(6) Mildew is caused by minute plants that grow from invisible seeds that float in the air. Where do we find mildew?

**Composition Exercise:** Tell the adventures of a dandelion seed as it flew away on the wings of a high wind.

**Drawing Exercise:** (1) Draw (*a*) a cluster of seed-balls of the plane tree; (*b*) a single seed (enlarged). (2) Draw the balloon of the dandelion (*a*) unbroken; (*b*) a single seed (enlarged to show that the seed is prickly) with its balloon.

# CHAPTER XXV

# How Plants Multiply Without the Help of Seeds

1. Of two bee-grubs exactly alike, one is placed by the bees into an ordinary cell, and, in due time, grows into a working bee; the other, placed in a larger cell and fed on richer food, comes out a queen bee! How it is done we do not know. In some similar way—though here, again, we know little—one plant-cell is so fed and placed as to become a stem-cell; another to become a leaf-cell. This stem-cell, again, may become a root-cell, and the leaf-cell may be so fed and placed as to become a thorn, a tendril, a sepal, a petal, a stamen, a pistil, a fruit!

2. We have already had examples showing how a leaf may disguise itself as a thorn or a tendril. Look at the flower of the bougainvillea, and you will see that the "flower" consists of coloured leaves. Examine, once more, a monthly rose that shows how the stamens turn into petals (fig. 109). Hold up a gooseberry to the light, and you will see that it is just a swollen leaf or leaves fitted for holding seeds.

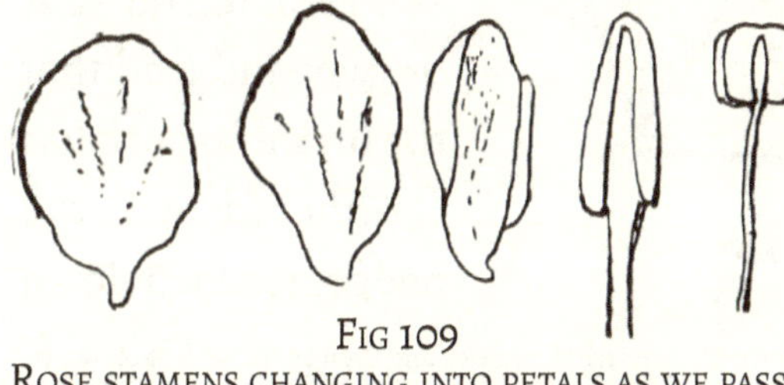

Fig 109

Rose stamens changing into petals as we pass from the centre of the rose outwards.

FIG 110
LEAVES GROWING OUT
OF A PINE-APPLE.

3. Indeed, in the pine-apple, as you know, the leaves push through the fruit and continue the growth upward. The same thing may now and then be seen in a rose-bloom. Pears, too, are sometimes found with a tuft of leaves growing out of the fruit.

4. **How a single leaf can make new plants.** There is a leaf that throws out roots at every notch of the edge when it is placed on damp, warm soil. In this way a crop of new plants may spring up all round the edge. The coleus and the beautiful begonias, so common in our plant-houses, are often multiplied by leaf-rooting.[41] Have you ever noticed the little plants that grow on the leaves of some ferns? Now and then, too, one finds little plants growing on the leaves of water-cress or cabbage.

5. **How a bramble goes on its travels.** Here is a little bramble plant four inches high, on the north side of a hedge ten feet high. We return in a year or two, and find that the bramble-bush has clambered over the hedge, reached down

FIG 111
BRAMBLE BUSH ROOTING.

41      Cut into the veins slightly where they are strongest, and then press the leaf on warm, moist earth. Do not bury the leaf.

on the other side, and rooted itself. A new bramble-bush from this root is stretching out its prickly fingers to seek new places where it may climb.

6. **How a little bit of leaf can make a whole plant.** A farmer with axe and spade roots up a hedge of prickly-pear. He carts it all away—root and stem and leaves. All? No; some small broken bits of the leaves are left on the loose earth. In a few months new plants are growing all along the line of the old hedge. The leaf-fragments have taken root!

7. **New plants may spring from roots.** And now, having seen how a plant may spring from a leaf, let us see what the root can do in multiplying plants. If you examine willow trees growing beside a river, you may often see a leafy shoot from a root that has been laid bare by the river. Cut off the root that bears the shoot and plant it, and you have a new tree. This sometimes happens when a flood bears off a root of this kind. Similarly, you may find a new plant growing from a raspberry root. If you dig up a raspberry plant that has not been touched for a season, you will probably find plants that have grown up from the roots, a foot or two away from the old plant.

8. **And the stem: can it, too, make new plants?** Yes, in a number of ways; sometimes from the stem above ground, and sometimes from the stem underground.

9. **How the stem above ground makes new plants.** Buffalo grass throws out long creeping stems, and at every joint of these a root may be formed. The couch grasses behave in the same way. All grasses of this class are said to root at the joint. When ground is loose, as at the sea-coast, these joint-rooting grasses can sometimes be taken up for unbroken lengths of ten

to twenty feet. It is with these long, creeping, rooting stems that the sand-grasses bind together the sand hills on the coastline.

10. **The runner that a strawberry-plant (fig. 112) sends out is just a creeping stem.** This has not gone far till it sends down a root; and from this a tuft of leaves rises to form a new plant.

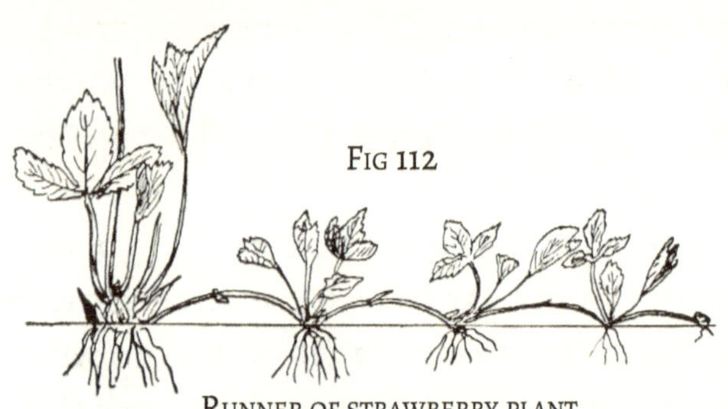



RUNNER OF STRAWBERRY PLANT.

Then it runs on a little further, and makes another plant. Give the runner time and good earth, and it will run in this way to the end of the longest bed. It is from the new plants on these runners that new beds of strawberries are planted out.

11. **Layering.** When you prune your gooseberry or currant bushes, you may often find hanging branches that have pushed themselves into the earth and formed new roots. Each of these may be planted out to form a new bush. Gardeners have learned by watching this plan to bend down the low branches of many other shrubs. They peg them into the ground, and then place a layer of earth over them. This method of growing a new plant is called **layering.**[42]

12. **Slips or cuttings.** If, instead of allowing a gooseberry branch to stoop to the earth and root itself, you cut off six or nine inches of ripened wood and plant it after the fall of the leaf, you will probably find that it takes root. There is enough ripe sap

42     The formation of roots will be more certain if a slight cut or twist be given to the part thus buried. The sap checked at the cut is rich in the forming matter that heals a wound or makes a root. In this case it does both.

in the wood to heal the wound and to throw out roots. Plants grown in this way are said to be grown from slips or cuttings.

13. **Underground stems.** In all the cases I have given, the stem or branch has grown in the air; but sometimes a stem does not rise into the air, but burrows in the ground.

14. **How underground stems make new plants.** Dig up a common bracken and you will see this burrowing stem. You see, too, where it is sending up shoots to form new plants. The **sucker** thrown up by a rose-bush is at first similar to a burrowing stem, but, after travelling a little way from the main stem, the sucker leaves the ground and becomes a new plant. The burrowing stem, on the other hand, after throwing up a new plant, goes on its way underground. The elm, the poplar, the plum, and the pear are among the trees that throw up suckers.

A NATIVE RUSH SHOWING THE GROWING ROOT.

15. **The tuber.** Sometimes the underground stem swells into a tuber, as in the potato. The potato that you eat is not really a root, but a part of the stem; and I need hardly say is not grown by the plant for our use but to make new plants. The "eyes" of the potato are just leaf-buds in the swollen stem.

16. **The bulb.** Sometimes, again, the underground stem swells out into a bulb. Very many of our spring wild flowers, like the Victorian crocus and the harbinger of spring, have bulbs.

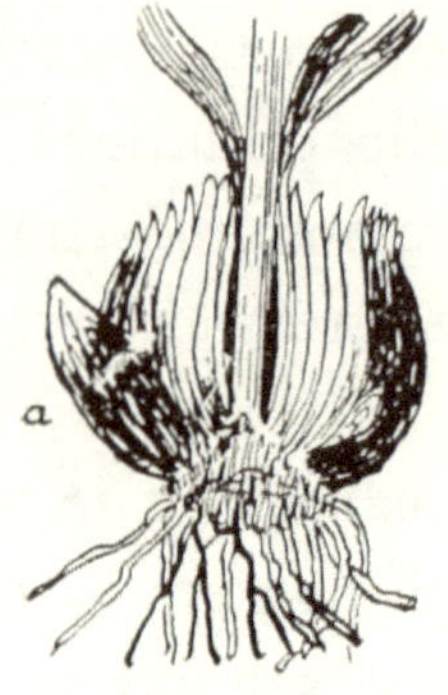

FIG. 114
SCALY BULB WITH
LITTLE BULBS (4, A)

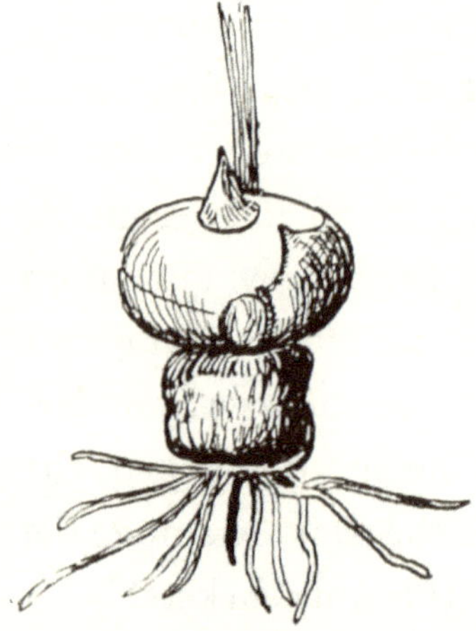

FIG. 115
SOLID BULB (GLADIOLUS)
SHOWING OLD WITHERED
BULB BELOW; THE NEW SOLID
BULB OF THIS YEAR'S BULB

Sometimes, as in the onion, the bulb can be broken up into thick scaly leaves. These scales, indeed, are just disguised leaves. Now, you know that in the angle between a leaf and the stem there is always a bud. The little bulbs, then, that form at the base of the scale-like leaves are just underground buds (fig. 114). Sometimes again, as in the gladiolus, the bulb is solid and cannot, like the onion, be broken up into scaly leaves. In such cases the little bulbs have to be formed above the old one, or at the side. Take up a bulb of the gladiolus, and you will often see the bulb of last year below the bulb of this year (fig. 115). You might think from this that in a year or two the bulb of the gladiolus would rise above ground; but, strange to say, such plants have the power to draw the bulb down into the ground, just as the roots of a bramble shoot that has touched the ground have power to draw down the shoot into the earth.

17. Among the wood sorrels introduced from South Africa into Australia, there is one with a pretty umbel of drooping yellow flowers. This plant is spreading fast by means of small bulbs that grow in large numbers on the long thread-like roots. Weeds, as a rule, are killed by being "turned in" in digging; but,

since digging scatters these little bulbs, it serves only to help the spread of this sorrel. A wood sorrel taken from South Africa to Malta has spread around the whole of the Mediterranean coast, not by seed but by small bulbs. This is probably the same plant.

18. **How man learned to be a gardener.** From all this you can see that Nature has many ways of multiplying plants besides scattering seed. You can see, too, how man has learned to follow Nature in this. He has watched and copied the plans of Nature. One man, in removing the leaves that had fallen below a begonia, chanced to notice that one of the leaves had rooted itself. The news spread, and, in a short time, all the gardeners in the world were growing begonias by leaf-rooting. It is in this way that man has learned to be a gardener.

Questions and Exercises:

(1)   Grow from cuttings the following: gooseberry, geranium, currant, rose, grape vine.

N.B. The cuttings should be of ripened wood planted after the autumn rains. Press earth firmly about the ends in the ground. The process of root-making may be watched if an ivy cutting be struck in water in a glass vase.

(2)   Get a strawberry plant from a strong runner. Plant in a bed where there is good soil and plenty of room on all sides. Note at the end of one year or two years how many new plants have grown from runners.

(3)   Grow buffalo or couch-grass from joints.

(4)   Grow two bulbs: one a scaly bulb (say the onion); the other a solid bulb (say the gladiolus). Note the different methods of bulb-multiplication.

(5)   If one of the green branches of a potato be covered with earth, it often forms a potato tuber. What does this prove?

(6)   Two ways of potato planting: (a) Since each eye is a bud, cut up the tuber, and plant as many seeds as there are eyes; (b) Plant a

whole tuber with only a single bud—a strong one—left. Which is likely to be the better plan? Remember that the starch stored in the tuber is to give the young plant a start.

(7)   Chop up a dock-weed root into bits and plant them. Note how many make new plants. Try similar experiments with sorrel-weed (sour grass).

NOTE: This will show why it is that plough and harrow do not destroy docks and sorrel weeds, but rather multiply them.

(8)   Remove all the leaves of a dandelion and see whether it can shoot afresh.

(9)   How do the following plants multiply without seed? Common sorrel-weed, peppermint, Danubian reed (bamboo), violet, verbena.

**Composition Exercise:** Tell how man learned to be a gardener.

**Drawing Exercise:** Show by a sketch how a strawberry-plant runs out to make new plants.

XXVI.

# How Plants Have Been Improved by Man

1. We have seen how man can bring the wild plants of all lands into his garden; and now we are to see how he can improve them. Man can make a poor plant into a fine plant, just as he can make a poor animal into a fine animal. Compare a dingo with a Scotch collie, and it will help you to see how much man has done to improve the wild dog. Compare the grass called wild oats with the oats of the farm, and you will see how man can improve a wild plant. It is easier to notice all this in an old country where you can see the wild plants side by side with the garden plants.

2. **From forest to orchard.** In parts of Europe you may pass in a few minutes from an autumn wood where the wild plum grows, to an orchard of plum trees; from the small harsh fruits of the sloe to the large juicy plums of the garden. Similarly, you may pass from the small fruit of the gean—the wild cherry—to the large fruit of a garden cherry-tree. So, also, we may pass from the crab—the wild apple—to the garden apple of a hundred kinds; and from the small strawberry of the woods to the large berry of the garden. You now know enough of plant-life to guess some of the ways in which these wonders have been

wrought. Here are a few hints to help you to think out the matter for yourselves.

3. **How the sloe was changed into the garden-plum.** (1) The tree was freed from all rivals—weeds and bushes and trees. (2) By frequent stirring, or by careful mulching,[43] the earth was kept open to rain and air. (3) Water was given when the rainfall was not enough. (4) Insect pests, which sometimes hurt the trees of the wood, were kept off. (5) The tree was regularly pruned. (6) Root-food was added to the soil when required.

4. In a similar way have our vegetables been improved. What a step, for example, from the wild cabbage of the coasts of England to the many kinds of cabbage and cauliflower that grow in our gardens!

5. **How the parsnip of to-day was raised.** The seed of the wild parsnip of England was sown in 1847 in an English garden. The soil was loose and rich; and only the very best of the seeds were saved from the very best of the plants. This choice of plant and seed was repeated, year after year, until the spindly, tough, strong-flavoured wild root became large and sweet. Then the seed of this garden-parsnip was sold all over the world by seedsmen. It is in this way also that we have improved the turnip, carrot,

Fig. 116
Parsnip

43    When the earth about a plant is kept open and moist by means of a litter of straw, or leaves, or other waste matter, it is said to be mulched. This is of special importance in Australia where the vegetable matter in the earth may be burned up by the hot sun. Darkness and moderate temperature, too, seem to be necessary to the bacteria that make root-food. All this raises questions as to the practice of "bare fallow" in a climate like ours.

Fig. 117
Sturt's desert pea

radish, and other vegetables (fig. 116).

6. As knowledge grows, some of our native plants may become garden vegetables. Our native spinach, sometimes called New Zealand spinach, is already used in this way.[44] Captain Cook made his men take this vegetable twice a day. You must not think, however, that we can take any wild plant and grow it in the garden. Some wild plants, like some wild birds, refuse to become garden pets. Try to grow any of your favourite wild flowers, and you may find this out. Sturt's desert pea is a good plant to try, because, with pains, you may succeed.[45]

7. **How the Wheat Plant is being improved.** More important than all these fruits and vegetables is the improvement man has made on the wheat plant. And still the work goes on. The wheat seeds of many lands are being tried in Australia to find the plant best suited for us. Nay, more; new kinds of wheat are being raised here to meet the needs of a new land and a new climate. The pollen blown from one kind of wheat to another

44      The Native Bower Spinach—a trailing plant very common on the Victorian coast—is also eatable, but is not so good a variety as the New Zealand Spinach, which is a native of New South Wales and Queensland.

45      The seed should be sown where the plants are to grow; on raised earth where the plants will not be disturbed and will not get any water except the rainfall. It is worth taking pains to grow this fine pea-flower (*Clianthus Dampieri*). It is named after Dampier, who found it in N.W. Australia in 1699, and presented a specimen to the British Museum. It was thus probably the first Australian flower to be seen in England.

may chance to make a valuable new plant; and man has copied Nature in this method of getting new kinds (fig. 117).

8. Let us say that a certain wheat is a great bearer and does not suffer much from the rust disease, but is too weak in the stalk to stand up against the spring gales. Then, if a flower of this wheat be dusted with the pollen of another good wheat that has a stout stalk, the seed may possibly give us a new wheat-plant with the good points of both kinds.

9. When you learn that from £2,000,000 to £3,000,000 are lost to Australia every year by rust in wheat, you will see how interesting and how important are problems of this kind.[46] In the same way, a dull-looking apple of good flavour may be crossed with an apple of handsome colour, in the hope that a new apple may be got that is good both in flavour and colour.

10. **From hedge-rose to garden rose.** Among the flowers, new kinds are being made in this way every year. Many of our best roses, indeed, are less than 20 years old; and hundreds of gardeners are still working at the problem of joining together in one rose the finest form, the finest colour, and the finest scent. The hedge-rose has a charm of its own, but what a distance separates it from *Maman Cochet* or the *Bride*! One of the greatest difficulties of the rose grower is to preserve scent in the improved rose.

11. **Improvement by budding and grafting.** Then there are the methods of improvement by budding and grafting. You are now able to understand those methods quite easily. We saw that a new bud is formed between every new leaf and the stem. By

46    The Governments of New South Wales and Victoria are working together over problems of this kind, and already with good results. See article in "The Journal of Agriculture," p. 415 by Mr. D. McAlpine.

the end of December, the new bud is generally ripe enough to be shifted from one tree to another.

12. **Budding.** First of all, you make a perpendicular slit about one inch long in the bark of the tree that is to receive the new bud. Do not go deeper than the bark. Then at the top of that slit make a cross-cut (fig. 118b); then, with a thin narrow paper-cutter or budding knife, raise the bark a little at each corner below the cross-cut.

Now we have to slice off the new bud. Slice off with a sharp knife, as shown in fig. 118, cutting off altogether an inch of bark and a very thin piece of wood with it. Then put the lower end of the bud into the cross-cut, and slide it down till the bud is a little below the cross-cut. Next, take a piece of soft, strong string or tape, and wind it around the bud from the bottom up. Wind the tape with a steady, tight but not hard strain, until you have covered the whole cut and left nothing in view but the bud. In a few days, the bud should have "taken." Recall the position of the leaf-sap tubes in the stem, and you will see at once how the leaf-sap runs into the new

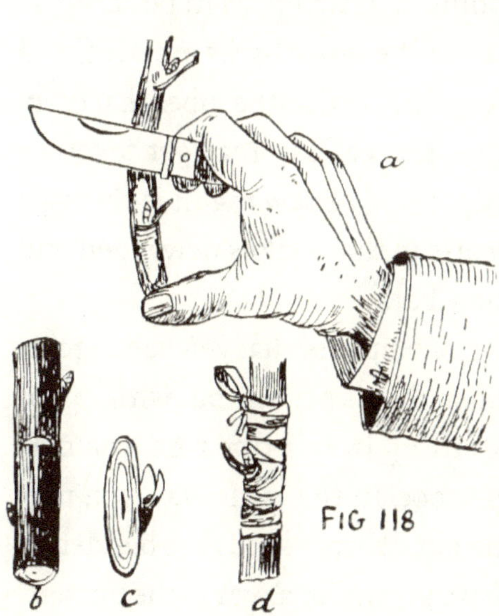



FIG. 118
BUDDING PROCESS
BUDDING TECHNIQUE SHOWING FOUR
STAGES: A: SLICING OFF THE BUD B:
BARK OPENED TO RECEIVE THE BUD
C: THE BUD READY FOR INSERTION D:
THE BUD INSERTED AND TIED UP

bud as if it belonged to the stem. You will also be able to understand the method of grafting which is shown in fig. 119.

13. **Grafting.** Grafting is done before the end of winter; instead of a bud we use a shoot of wood of last summer's growth. The branch that is to receive this shoot is cut as shown in fig. 119a, and the shoot b is cut so as to fit in exactly. Next, some clay or grafting wax is plastered on, and the whole is then bound up with tape. The great point in grafting, as in budding, is to get the inner barks exactly fitted together, so that the tubes that carry the ripe leaf-sap may get together (fig. 119). We saw that it is this ripe leaf-sap that makes new wood and new bark.

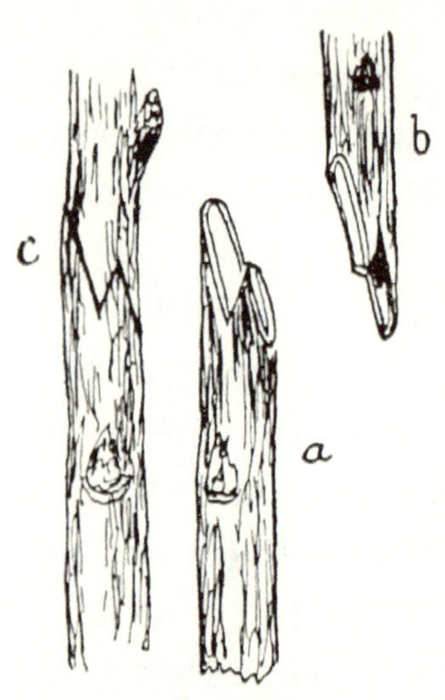


FIG. 119
GRAFTING TECHNIQUE WHERE: B IS TO BE GRAFTED ON A THE NOTCH IN THE STOCK FITS EXACTLY IN THE SLIT IN THE BARK OF THIS ONE C SHOWS THE GRAFT IN PLACE

14. Suppose that you have a rose-bush that is healthy but with a poor flower; then by budding or grafting from a fine rose, you may get a good flower on a strong root. In the same way, you may improve your fruit-trees. Fine but delicate kinds are budded or grafted on strong kinds that have grown for a year in the nursery. Apples that suffer from the apple-aphis are grafted or budded on roots that are proof against this pest; and trees that cannot stand a damp soil are grown on roots that thrive in such soil.

15. Of all the plans for improving plants, the simplest for you to try is that of sowing the best seeds of the best plants.

Wonderful improvements have been made in this way. And here again, we are but copying Nature. Let us suppose that 100 seeds fall from an annual, and that all these get covered with earth. Most of the seeds come up, but after a struggle one plant only remains. Which one? Some of the seeds grew on the strong well-sunned shoots of the annual, and others on weak or shaded shoots. Some, therefore, of the seeds would be stronger than the others, and of the strong seeds, one might be strongest of all. The plant from this seed smothers the rest! The gardener, when he picks the best seed, is but copying Nature.

NOTE.—Scholars in wheat-growing districts might make experiments in improving the seed-wheat. The plan is to sow selected seeds in a seed plot, and the following year again to select the best heads and again sow in a separate plot. This process is continued for a few years. The results obtained in this way in Canadian schools have been so valuable that 450 of the parents (in farming districts) have formed a society for producing pure-bred seed by hand selection.

### Questions and Exercises.

(1) After midsummer, make experiments in budding. N.B. Strong-growing rose and peach trees with bark that lifts readily are easily budded. If the budding be done early in summer, the strong sap-flow makes the bud push out a shoot, and this shoot is likely to be weak. It is better that the bud remain dormant till the following spring.

(2) During winter, make experiments in grafting. Note: if some cuttings of cherry plum have been planted the previous winter, they will now be ready for grafting upon. For experiments in pear-tree growing, suckers from a pear-tree can be planted in the nursery during the previous winter. Pupils should be warned, however, that

pear-trees grown on suckers are apt to sucker freely. Good growers raise their pear stocks from seed.

(3) One often sees suckers of a wild plum growing from the roots of a garden plum, or the suckers of a wild cherry growing from a garden cherry. Explain.

(4) Should experiments in crossing be tried, two points must be noted: (a) the flower must be operated on as soon as open; (b) after being fertilised, the flower must have a small bag of muslin tied round it to keep off insects. Dahlias make good subjects for experiment. For fine work, a camel-hair brush may be used for transferring pollen.

**Composition exercise:**—Tell how weeds have been turned into garden vegetables, and wild fruits into garden fruits.

**Drawing exercise:**—Draw a hedge rose, and, alongside of it, your favourite garden rose.

XXVII.

# How One Season Prepares for the Next

1. Some plants, like the poppy or the garden pea, die before winter comes; others, like the carrot, live for two seasons; and others, again, like the oak tree, live for many years.

2. **Annuals, biennials, and perennials.** The plants that live for one season only are called **annuals**. Such a plant is the portulaca. The portulaca puts out its beautiful white, pink, red, or yellow flowers in the hot months; and so you need not sow the seed you have saved till the winter is quite over. This plant, then, disappears entirely from Victoria at the end of summer. No trace of the plant remains, and, but for the tiny shining seeds that glisten in the seed-cup, we should have no more portulaca.

3. The plants that live on through the winter for one more season are called **biennials**. Such are the carrot, turnip, and other vegetables that spend one season in storing up food in order that they may flower in the second year. Plants that live on, year after year, like the oak, are called **perennials**. Compare a red gum that was a great tree when William the Norman set foot in England with a Shirley poppy that lives for four months, and you will see what a step we have made in passing from the annual to the perennial.

**4. How trees begin in spring to prepare for next spring.** Having looked at the seeds that carry the life of the annual from one season to another, we have now to see how trees and other perennials get ready for next spring. If you look at the place where a leaf is joined to the stem, you will find a bud. It looks as if it were hiding between the leaf-stalk and the stem. In these buds are wrapped up the shoots or the flowers of next year. Even in early spring you can see the tiny buds in which lie hid the shoots and flowers of the following spring! Twelve months before they are needed, the tree begins to get them ready. All through the summer they grow, and by autumn-time they have swollen so much that they help to push off the leaves that have guarded them against cold and heat.

Have you ever noticed how well the rose leaf protects its bud?

**5. How young buds are protected.** Pluck a rose leaf and you will see that the base of the leaf-stalk is winged. These wings for protecting the bud are called stipules. Not every plant has stipules, and some that have stipules soon lose them. In others, like the rose and the common garden pea, the stipules do not fall off, but remain to protect the new bud. When stipules are absent, you will often find that the leaf-stalk is hairy or broadened out at the base so as to protect the little bud. Sometimes, as in the bougainvillea, a thorn serves the same purpose. By

Compound leaf of rose, with stipules connecting the young bud

the time the leaf falls and the bud is left bare, it is hardy enough to bear the night-cold.

6. **The fall of the leaf.** When winter draws near, the leaf gives up its starch to be stored away in the inner bark, and then the leaf-stalk is gradually cut off from the currents of sap. A layer of cork is made to cover over each sap-tube just where it enters the leaf-stalk. In this way the flow is stopped, and when the leaf falls there is no "bleeding" from the wound. Break off a leaf of a Virginia creeper that is red for the fall and you will see the corky layers clearly.

7. When the leaves fall, the bare buds show so plainly against the autumn sky that you wonder that you never noticed them earlier in the season. You need not blame yourself, for they are not easily seen. Sometimes, indeed, it is impossible to see the bud until the leaf falls. Such is the case in the plane tree, which beautifies so many of our streets.

FIG. 121
LEAF OF PLANE TREE, SHOWING
THE CUP THAT HIDES THE
BUD DURING SUMMER

8. **Puzzle: find the plane tree bud!** In the plane, the base of the leaf-stalk is hollowed out so as to form a kind of cup which completely covers the bud. Before the fall of the leaves, you puzzle yourself to find the buds for next year. No buds! What a puzzling tree!

9. **What is inside a bud?** Remove gently with a pin the smooth outer cap, and you uncover a gummy cap that glis-

tens in the sunshine. This gum helps to keep the bud warm, and it serves also as a waterproof coat. Below the gummy cap comes a cloak covered with rich golden-brown hairs. Then come hairs, and more hairs, till it seems as if the bud were wrapped up like an Arctic traveller. Then we have another cloak, and then the first glimpse of the coming leaves.

10. If you can now get a large flower-bud of the white poplar, you will see a bud of another kind. Here, instead of caps, we have scales, small and large; more scales than in the plane tree bud, but no gum. At last we come to the flower-cone, snugly sleeping under a thick coverlet of beautiful white silky hair. We shall never wonder again that buds can defy the frosts of a winter night. They are as snug and warm as a kitten under its mother's fur.

11. **How the beauty of spring lies hid in the bud.** Here, then, in these little buds, lie shoot and flower, ready, with the spring sunshine, to break into branch and blossom. Now you can understand how it is that in some backward seasons spring comes with a rush of leaf and flower. Spring does not make the leaf and the flower; all it does is to open the buds. The spring sun sets the sap flowing briskly; the bud swells and throws off its many coats, and then the green shoot breaks out into the light!

12. **How the bulbs get ready for next spring.** Some of the bulbs, too, like the Victorian crocus, are already in autumn almost prepared to thrust up their leaves and flowers. Indeed, in some mild autumns, a few peep above the ground before winter comes, as if they had made a mistake in the season. When a small-seeded plant, like a poppy, comes up, it has to work hard with root and leaf before it can gather strength

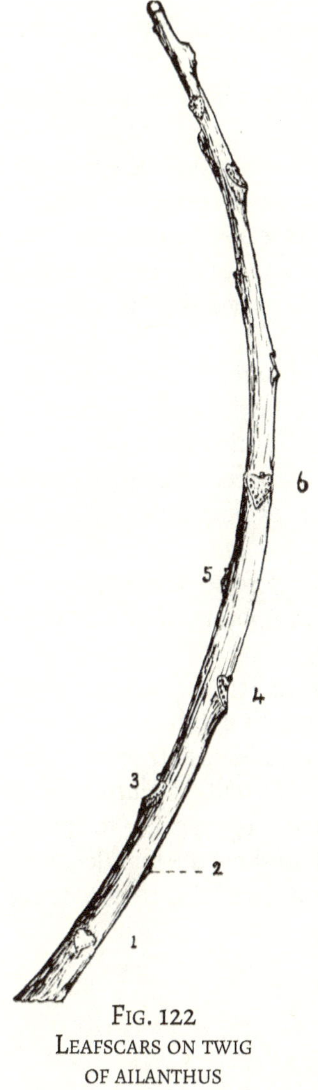



FIG. 122
LEAFSCARS ON TWIG
OF AILANTHUS

enough to make a flower; but the bulbs that got this work done in the previous season are ready to flower at once. The bulbs have money in the Savings Bank and so can afford to have a gay dress without waiting to earn the cost. This is why most of our early spring flowers are bulbs.

As autumn advances, a litter of leaves gathers under the English trees. These fallen leaves make the finest of manure. How much richer the soil of Australia might be today if our gum trees had been shedding their leaves every autumn for ages past! As the leaves fall, we can see a dozen things that we could not see when the leaves were on the trees—the plan of the branching, the leaf scars new and old, the twig-galls, the witches' brooms, the ridges that show where the rivers of sap met, and the birds' nests of last spring. Above all, we see against the pale blue of the winter sky the beautiful network of twig and branch.

Each season has its own charm. And if we bring to Nature each year a finer heart and a fuller mind, the charm of each season will deepen with each year of our lives.

<u>Questions and Exercises.</u>

(1) Examine the stipules of the hawthorn, dahlia, pear, common garden pea.

(2) Note how the stipules act as rain and dew-holders in the pansy, dock, rhubarb.

(3) Show how pine-trees are fitted to bear a fall of snow; and holly-trees; and the New Zealand coprosma (looking-glass plant).

(4) Pull a leaf from any tree that sheds its leaves annually, and look at (a) the leaf-scar left on the stem, (b) the scars of the previous year, (c) still older scars. *Note.*—Leaf-scars show very clearly in ailanthus (see fig. 122).

(5) The wild geranium, which is an annual in Europe, tends to become a perennial here. The root has become thicker, and this store of food carries the plant over the winter. Examine the root.

(6) Note the beauty of the twigs of English trees when seen against the winter sky. Compare the outer branches of the elm with those of the oak.

(7) In a split cabbage you see, on a large scale, the interior of a bud. Note the stem tapering to its growing point and the crowded crumpled layers.

(8) In fig. 122, the numbers show that the 6th bud is directly over the first bud. Examine a number of trees, and find if this plan of bud is a common one among plants that have two seed-leaves (Dicotyledons).

**Composition exercise:**—Tell the story of a bud—a plum-tree bud if you have any plum-trees in your district—from spring to spring.

**Drawing Exercise:**—Draw a rose leaf, to show the stipules. Draw (a) a leafless tree in outline; (b) a small branch of this tree in detail.

# SUMMARIES

### I. HOW SEEDS GERMINATE.—Part I.

1-5. A seed with two seed-leaves: the French bean: its plantlet. 6. How to watch seeds while germinating: use moist sawdust or a glass tube, filled with sawdust, in a pot of earth. 7. The soil. 8. A large plantlet: castor-oil. 9. The little root in the seed. 10. The seed-leaves: two bean-halves. 11. The true leaves. 12. Three needs in germination: heat, moisture, and air.

### II. HOW SEEDS GERMINATE.—Part II

1-3. A seed with one seed-leaf: wheat: the plantlet. 4-5. How a wheat-seed grows. 6. The veins in the leaves. 7. The roots. 8. The root-tip. 9. When this is injured, new roots grow out from the wounded root.

### III. THE ROOT.—Part I.

1-3. The root feeds by drinking: takes in fluids only: all the materials needed by the tree are borne hither by water. 4-5. Water climbs up a tree through the plant cells, and is helped up by the evaporation taking place through the leaves. 6-7. Two experiments: to prove that the root lifts water: grape-vine; balsam. 8-9. The fluid passes into the root-cell because the fluid there is stronger than the earth fluid. 10. Salt in soil may draw the fluid out of the root. 11. An imitation plant-cell. 12. Most of the food a root consumes moves through the leaves, but the material it brought remains in the plant.

### IV. THE ROOT.—Part II.

1-2. The root shuns the light, yet keeps near the surface. 3. Roots seek the best drinking places. 4. But they avoid sodden ground. 5. The hairs on the root take in food. 6. Some plants have trained themselves to live in wet ground. 7. The changing the water level affects the habits of plants.

## V. THE ROOT.—Part III.

1-2. Tap-roots and fibrous roots. 3. Fleshy roots. 4. Roots from creeping stems. 5. Reasons for different root shapes. 6-7. Nature is continually renewing the foods needed by the roots. 8-12. The good farmer imitates Nature by using manure and adopting rotation of crops. 13-14. Various tiny creatures (bacteria) also assist the roots by keeping the soil airy and drained.

## VI. THE STEM.—Part I.

1-2. The stem supports the leaves and flowers, and acts as a channel for the sap. 3-6. Growth of the stem: the heart-wood; the new stem-wood; the bark; ringing. 7. Comparison of one-and two-year old stems. 8-10. Root-sap and leaf-sap and their tubes. 11. The silver-grain and pith-rays.

## VII. THE STEM.—Part II.

1-2. The sap-tubes. 3-5. Experiments to show the water-path in stem and leaf: vine shoot (two seed-leaves); Danubian reed (one seed-leaf). 6-7. Palms and reeds grow by adding new growth at the top. 8. How a tree ringed half-way round behaves.

## VIII. CLIMBING PLANTS AND PARASITES.

1. Plants seek light. 2. Scrambling plants: rose, bramble. 3-4. Twining plants: hop, honeysuckle, and convolvulus: one winds one way faster than the other. 5. Twining stems buried in wood. 6. Tendrils: Virginia creeper, Japanese ivy, grape vine. 7. Air-root plants: ivy. 8-11. Plants living on the juices of other plants: mistletoe, dodder, mushroom, rust. 12. The gardener imitates this scheme of Nature by budding and grafting.

## IX. THE LEAVES.—Part I

1-7. Plants try to get as much as possible of carbon-dioxide, a gas breathed out by man and made by every fire and light; but forming only a small proportion of the air. 8-9. Leaves without light cannot take in this air-food. 10-12. Plants turn towards the sunlight.

## X. THE LEAVES.—Part II.

1–4. Plants are built up mostly from air and water, and the solid food contained in the latter. 5. They turn dead stuffs, like carbon and lime, into living foods. 6. The leaf cannot travel to seek food. 7-10. The leaf under the microscope: upper skin of water cells; two rows of long cells below, where the stuff of which the plant is built are made; looser cells where water leaves the leaf through breathing-pores in the lower skin.

## XI. THE LEAVES.—Part III

1-2. Starch in a potato. 3-4. A white leaf can make no starch. 4. Nor can one that gets no sunlight. 5-6. The sun force at work in a plant. 7-8. The leaf uses up carbon and gives out oxygen. 9-10. Experiment to show that leaves give off water.

## XII. LEAVES—SHAPES AND VEIN-PLANS.

1-2. The leaf-stalk; rarely round. 3-4. The leaf-blade: flat, and broad; long and narrow; network of leaflets; appearance on each side. 5. The stalk-plan: single-veined. 6. How the root-sap spreads over the leaf. 7. How the leaf-sap returns to the stem. 8-13. Shapes: feather-like, palm-like; entire, saw-edged, toothed, lobed, dissected; heart, egg, spear-head, arrow-head, hair-like, shield, etc. 14. Opposite leaves; the whorl. 15. Smooth, hairy, rough, soft, velvety. 16. Simple, compound.

## XIII. LEAVES—REASONS FOR LEAF SHAPES.

1-3. The grass-leaf type: one seed-leaf. 4-6. How light shapes the leaves: narrow in scanty light. 7. How the leaves differ on the same plant. 8. The original home of the tree must be considered; umbrella-tree. 9-10. Plants that alter their leaves as they grow older: gum-tree. 11. The first leaves of the black-wood tree. 12. How sap flows shapes the leaf: ivy. 13. Leaves that catch flies; sundew.

## XIV. HOW LEAVES PROTECT THEMSELVES.

1-3. How leaves are protected from cold; clover, gum sapling. 5-6. Protection from heat; by storing water, e.g., purslane, stonecrop, cactus; by checking loss of water, through hard skin, curled leaves, salted sap, hairy coat, or spray of perfume. 7-10. How leaves are guarded against animals: by sting; flat, dandelion; by unpleasant taste; by thorns, spines and hairs, gorse, thistles.

## XV. THE FLOWER—WHAT IS A FLOWER?

1-8. The flower is a seed-maker; it is not always coloured; nor is it always scented. 9. Flowers have different plans for making seeds; colour, scent, insects, birds, winds are in turn used, while some flowers dust their own seed-case with their own dust.

## XVI. THE PARTS OF A FLOWER.

1. Protection of scarlet geranium. 2-3. The flower-stalk; why is it high or low, why is it hairy? 4. The green sheath of the flower-cluster. 5. How the younger flower-buds are protected by the older flowers. 6. The calyx; sepals; a shield and a support. 7. The corona, petals. 8-9. The honey-tube.

## XVII. THE PARTS OF A FLOWER (continued).

1-4. The stamens bear the pollen cases or anthers which dust the insects with pollen. 4. The pistil and stigma. 5-6. The seed-case or ovary; seeds. 7. The seed is thrown into the air by curling elastic stalks. 8. Plants with two seed-leaves generally have five-fold flowers; one seed-leaf gives three-fold flowers.

## XVIII. THE GERANIUM'S DEBT TO INSECTS.

1-3. The geranium, like most of the finest flowers, sends its pollen to other geranium flowers and gets their pollen in return. 4. Mixture of flowers gives strength and beauty. 5-7. The long flower-stalk and the gay colour attract insects. 8. The petal door-step. 9. Guides to the honey-tube; grooves. 10-11. The hairs and oil that brush honey-thieves. 12. The geranium can make its seed properly only in South Africa, its native country. 13. Weeds using their own pollen spread widely and rapidly. All the gay flowers do not need insects. 14. Rain injures pollen.

## XIX. REGULAR AND IRREGULAR FLOWERS.

1. Tubular flowers. 2. Regular and irregular flowers. 3-7. Petals of irregular flowers are planned to suit insects: the snapdragon's mouth and the humble bee; the lip-flowered family, salvias, lavender, mint, thyme. 8. How the salvia dusts the bee with pollen. 9-10. Structure of the gorse flower. 11. A bee in the gorse flower. 12. Structure of the white clover. 13. The clover bee.

## XX. MORE ABOUT THE FLOWERS' DEBT TO INSECTS.

1-2. Honey-guides. 3-5. Hairs and sticky patches act as guards to the honey. 6. The different position of the honey-stores in different plants. 7-8. The charm and the mystery of scent. 9-11. The colour of flowers: stamens become petals that grow gay in colour; yellow, pink, purple, blue, white. 12. How the bees paint flowers. 13. An increase of bees may give gayer colours to our native flowers.

## XXI. WIND-FERTILIZED FLOWERS.

1-2. The oak uses the wind to scatter its seed over the tree. 3. The poplar has the pollen flower in one tree, the pistil flowers on another. 4. The pollen is generally made and scattered before the leaves come out. 5-6. How the common plantain scatters its seed. 7-8. The wheat and maize plants.

## XXII. HOW SEEDS ARE SPREAD.

1-2. Only a small proportion of seeds become plants. 3. Krakatoa was restocked with plants by winds, waves, and birds. 4-6. Some plants jerk their seeds out of the fruit: geranium, field-sorrel, gorse, dolichos. 7-8. Wattle and other smells are spread by water. 9. The coco-nut is carried to distant lands by ocean currents. 10. Pondweeds and seaweeds throw off little buds, borne along on the surface of the water. 11. Some grasses bury their seeds by means of bristles or awns.

## XXIII. HOW SEEDS ARE SPREAD BY ANIMALS.



## XXIV. HOW SEEDS ARE CARRIED BY THE WIND.



## XXV. HOW PLANTS MULTIPLY

## WITHOUT THE HELP OF SEEDS.



## XXVI. HOW PLANTS HAVE BEEN IMPROVED BY MAN.

## XXVII. HOW ONE SEASON PREPARES FOR THE NEXT.

1-3. Annuals, portulaca; biennials, carrot, turnip; perennials, gun tree, oak. 4. How trees begin in spring to prepare for next spring: buds. 5. How young buds are protected: stipules, hairy bud-stalk, thorn. 6-7. The fall of the leaf. 8. The plane-tree bud is hidden in a cup during summer. 9-11. The inside of a bud. 12. How the bulbs get ready for next spring. The peculiar charm of each season.